ENDURING

Stories of Unconditional Love

edited by

Brianne DiMarco

BLUE FORGE PRESS

Port Orchard ✹ Washington

Dedicated to everyone who has
(without complaint or regret)
sacrificed for love.

Acknowledgments

Blue Forge Press thanks author David Martyn who brought this idea to us (and whose story closes this collection) and all the authors—both established and brand new—who contributed stories to *Enduring*.

Some of the stories you'll find in these pages were the first ever written by the authors. Others are tales crafted after decades of writing professionally. This is at the heart of what we do: Bringing diverse storytellers together and lifting them up together.

May we all continue to blur the lines and break out of boxes that keep us separate. Ultimately, we are all here on this beautiful earth together for a brief time... let us spend that time embracing love.

Table of Contents

ENDURING

Stories of

Unconditional Love

HOW I LEARNED TO LOVE MYSELF

by Stacey Venzel

My heart hurts, a wrenching pain with each beat. My pulse is hurried; my inhales choppy, arrhythmic, panicked. Exhales are my only short-lived salvation. I feel like I'm suffocating. I am having an anxiety attack.

I cannot pinpoint my first bout with anxiety, cannot trace it back to its hasty, surprising beginning. I do know that I haven't always had it. I do know that it got worse—way worse—before it got better. I also know that I struggled with it long before I knew what it was.

Learning to view this as a courageous battle and not something born out of weakness was one of the most difficult paths on the road toward knowing, accepting, and loving myself.

These days, I know myself better than I ever thought I could know another living being. I know my wants and needs, my desires and aspirations. I can label my triggers and sort through my trauma. I understand my body's quirks, its struggles and triumphs. I can honor my flaws in a manner that supports me reaching my highest potential.

And above all, I know that I am worthy. I am enough.

But the journey toward this revelation was rife with sacrifices, some easier than others—all necessary.

The end result of loving myself did not start with a thirst for knowledge, no yearning to reach my inner depths, no intentions to set foot down an arduous path of soul-searching. Embarkation on the self-love train may have even planted its roots when I was young. But in the same sense that it did not have a conscious beginning, it neither had an accidental one. Like many parts of life, it just sort of happened. From there was laid the groundwork for me to embrace or ignore the opportunity. Ultimately, the reflection of all that I sacrificed was more powerful and meaningful than the sacrifices themselves. Perhaps it reached the point where I sacrificed until the sacrifices were no longer sacrifices. Perhaps.

———————

Every year in Catholic elementary school, each student in my class gave something up for the season of Lent. The traditional Lenten promise has three tenets, that of prayer, fasting, and almsgiving. While fasting from food is still a custom in various capacities among numerous Catholic households, the cultural norm has shifted more toward abstention from luxuries and vices, which may include activities.

As a child, I began to find that giving up things like ice cream or watching TV were not as difficult as a commitment to do something, and thus kick-started the evolution of my Lenten sacrifice toward giving up my time.

I live a frugal life, both selectively and out of financial necessity, yet I have experienced the hard truth that money comes back and time doesn't. Growing into adulthood, time is a greater sacrifice for me. Coming to this realization hugely shifted my socializing—in addition to my yearly Lenten promise—into a more manageable, more self-forgiving lifestyle.

I didn't realize until I was 28 years old how important it is to make time for yourself.

———————————

FOMO is real and I didn't realize I had it until I was too tired—too depressed—to do things. To do anything.

It's the Fear Of Missing Out, of hearing about all the fun, so much fun, your friends had the night before when you either chose not to join them or couldn't because you already had plans. FOMO is so very real that it led me to over-commit, to double-book, to party-hop, and to never, ever be alone in my apartment.

———————————

The loneliness is settling in. My phone screen has not shown any new text notifications all day. I am craving human touch, human voices, but I am so very, very tired. I pick up my phone and select a friend in my contact list. The line rings. There is no answer.

I select another name from the saved contacts. Again, the line rings. Again, there is no answer.

I live with a roommate who I never see and so, for all intents and purposes, I live alone. I am single. I am unsure if I am still heartbroken. I feel lonely. I am alone.

———————————

One is a state of being, the other a state of mind.

I was 21 years old when I began to understand that being alone and feeling alone are, in fact, two very different states.

It was my first solo trip abroad, traversing a foreign

land in my non-native tongue, holding tight to the backpacks strapped to my chest and back. It was isolation in the Amazon rainforest, a primitive cohabitation with tarantulas, scorpions, cockroaches, and fourteen strangers from seven different countries. It was grueling, hot, sweaty manual labor. It was feeling violated when I was robbed, then feeling lost without my belongings or network of trusted loved ones. And then it was feeling alone.

———————————

I would go on to travel to nearly two dozen more countries by myself in the decade that followed. I would go on to seek the unknown, to drop myself into a place where I knew nothing and no one and only left when I knew something and someone. I would go on these adventures that dangled overhead that feeling of loneliness, always within reach. I would go on to be comfortable being with strangers, and I would go on to be comfortable—happy even—being alone.

———————————

I am in a crowded room yet feel alone, a dichotomous feat that many have experienced yet fewer have dissected. That feeling of loneliness stems from who I have surrounded myself with: so-called friends who have proven to be unreliable, family members who seep dishonesty and ungratefulness, co-workers who shed toxicity to my well-being.

To be alone, physically and mentally, gives me the space to think, think, and over-think. Thinking is beneficial—can be beneficial—but I can't turn it off. My mind is a prison holding my body captive.

And it begins to pick apart my flaws.

———————————

In 2011, I was diagnosed with Lyme disease after six months of dwelling inside human flesh with bones that did not seem like they belonged to me. In the ensuing months and years after treatment, I battled arthritic-like pain daily. I pushed through the discomfort every waking day. I twice tried training for my dream marathon. I twice had to call it quits.

I hated my body.

―――――――――――

I once went three months without using a mirror. I saw my physical appearance only in tide pools, the metal convex back of the spoon, and window panes. I wore no make-up. My clothing choices were limited to the contents of a duffel bag.

Instead of focusing on how my body looked, I shifted focus to how my body felt. Did it feel healthy and well-rested? Were there any aches and pains? I became incredibly in-tune with every creaking joint and headache. I learned to be patient with my body. I accepted that it had its limitations. And I found a balance between pushing myself and listening to my body.

―――――――――――

As much as I hated my body, I also hated my mind. I wanted to rewire my neurons and synapses so I wouldn't feel so deeply all the things that I feel―pain, shame, anger, annoyance, sadness, hope, love... even happiness.

I get so excited about the little things. I love that about myself now but felt judged by too many for so long for how joyful I can be. Now, maybe, I see that they were jealous. Maybe. Of how carefree I can be―at least on the outside, trying to be on the inside.

―――――――――――

I've just read a news story about strangers that brings me to tears―tears on the inside, tears on the outside. Happy tears. Now I read another, also about strangers, also bringing me to tears. Sad tears, angry tears.

I am emotional. I cry with gratitude snuggling my guinea pig because her simple existence makes me wonder how I got so lucky to have her in my life. I cry when one of my students says something so cute and innocent and pure, and cry again when I learn of another student's hardships. I cry when someone is mad at me, when I am treated unjustly, when I feel loved and unloved. I cry when I'm having a difficult conversation and am trying to process it all.

Years of therapy taught me self-compassion, taught me to embrace my emotional self, taught me that I am an empath. Therapy taught me how to process my emotions, the workings of my mind, the workings of myself.

An empath feels what another is feeling, so deeply that it leaves an open wound that will fester for days before it heals. I used to think this was a curse that impeded me from finding the pockets of joy in an overwhelmingly inhumane world. Could it, though, truly be a gift?

I've seen my students quickly shift from participating in the group activity to explosively throwing themselves on the floor, snot escaping from their noses, tears trailing down their cheeks, shrieks echoing from their lungs.

My students remind me of my childhood self, always putting too much pressure on accomplishing tasks to perfection, inevitably leading to frustration. They remind me of my adult self, too.

My students are not overly sensitive. They are not too sensitive. They are just more sensitive, while others are less sensitive. They taught me that it isn't just children who are learning to manage and regulate their emotions, but adults as well. They also taught me that it's okay to have your feelings as well as to let others have theirs.

Each of my five senses is awakened as I feel—deeply feel—these feelings I'm feeling.

I am crushed, in too many senses of the word. My body is folded in on itself, curled up in the fetal position, arms cradling legs in a maternal, self-comforting way. My future, once colorful and hopeful, is now a blurry streak of grays and blacks and whites. My eyes must have an anvil pushed against them, for there is no other way to explain the pressure my tears have caused.

Fighting for myself does not come as easily as fighting for others does. I am confident in my abilities but timid in my undertaking. For too long, I have been a pushover, picking up the slack of others, making excuses for people because I choose to see the good in them. Then comes a time when I am sinking, not swimming, and I know I have to turn the tides. No one is fighting for me, and no one will fight for me—unless that someone is me.

It is time to remove the anvil.

I am underpaid. I am overworked. I am mistreated. I am contracted to follow the rules. I am not here to break the rules. I am here to make new rules. I am respectful despite being disrespected. I am honest despite all the dishonesty. I am valuable, and I am being taken advantage of.

The future me is calling, and it is telling me now is the time. Now is the time to fight for myself.

And so I will, and so I do. I fight for myself.

My friend tells me I should have given the middle finger when I walked out that door, that I shouldn't have stayed once I told them the end was near, that I did not need to stick around.

I asked my friend why, after knowing when the end was, I put so much effort into what I left behind, into making things easy for a place and for people that made things so horrible for me. My friend said I did it because that's who I am.

I think I'm beginning to understand now.

———————————

I'm beginning to understand my worth. I am starting to become so incredibly self-aware that I can't cough without knowing why I coughed, can't get a headache without knowing what caused the headache.

I'm beginning to understand my feelings, and how my past shaped my present, is shaping my future.

I'm beginning to understand who I want in my life, who my real friends are, who is good for me.

And so I begin to shed the toxicity, so that I may nourish and flourish and blossom into the woman I choose to be.

———————————

I couldn't wait to show you the results of a year of hard, dedicated, isolated work. I couldn't wait to hear you say you were proud of me when you held those results in your very own hands and read the personalized inscription. I didn't expect you to point out the mistakes, to laugh in my face when I did something so unlike me and stood up for myself.

I believe in the good of humanity. I really do. But some people in my life—in everyone's life—are just rude, offensive, and cruel. Some people are spiteful and hold grudges. Some people focus on pulling me down instead of lifting me up.

Some people just have to go.

———————————

I thought cutting ties with someone who played a meaningful part in the workings of my life would leave a permanent mark, a scar that I would pick at but could never erase. But I had the power to make that person's significance insignificant to my story, because sometimes the meaningful part a person played in my life was not due to love and compassion but rather selfishness and greed. Sometimes that person was only significant because of the changes that ensued, evolved, as a result of the interactions we shared, the changes that I took upon myself to create.

I have spent a great deal of time agonizing over relationships with people who do not treat me how I both want to be treated and deserve to be treated. Because I give people second, third, fourth, and fifth chances, I have, in the past, blinded myself to the core truth of some of my relationships with individuals. I have called people friends when they have time and again left me waiting for hours on a brilliantly sunny day, wasting away my precious free time, just waiting, waiting, waiting for them to show up. Like they said they would. Sometimes they do. Sometimes they don't.

Some people just have to go.

I needed you, needed them. I was fighting one trauma I didn't know I'd experienced and another that wouldn't stop rattling my bones just like it did for 36 hours straight in the now, and for weeks in the then.

I needed you, needed them. I reached out and found hope in words spoken, then disappointment in commitments not followed through. Those friendships, it seems, were ones out of convenience; those words, it seems, were false promises made out of care and concern but without a full heart's backing. Those people, it seems, wouldn't last in my life forever; the trauma, it seems, would.

It's been four years but I can still feel the terror when I close my eyes and remember. I was terrified before, I was terrified during, and I was terrified after. My eyes are raw from crying; my stomach is twisted from holding back vomit. I recall my own fear, and I recall their fear. I cannot shake the unpredictability, the unexpectedness, the unpreparedness. I cannot erase the scenes of the apocalyptic aftermath.

But I see the beauty and resilience that shined through it all.

What am I without a sense of community? Asking for help, it seems, does not make me weak. Leaning on others, it seems, is not a mistake.

This is the community I've been seeking. This is the community that rose from the rubble. This is the community that looked down the barrel of fear together. This is the community that will—would—overcome the destruction, the terror, and the fear.

Fear: a feeling I know well enough to call a kindred spirit, one that hovers above me, sidled up next to me when I rode the bus then and sidles up next to me when I ride the bus now. Courage: my ability to overcome it.

Courage, it seems, is not fearlessness. It is feeling that overwhelming feeling of fear and going up against it. It is not shying away from an exhausting, terrifying battle that I might lose because sometimes those fears are real.

Sometimes those fears are perceived. And facing them is often harder than facing the real ones.

Choosing to love someone is a leap of faith. It is anxiety-inducing because I cannot predict how it will turn out. It is a fear faced every day throughout the world, a relatable fear that sometimes has happy endings, but sometimes does not.

Choosing to love myself—committing to loving myself—is an unpredictable journey, but one I hoped—hope—would—will—have a happy ending.

––––––––––––

What do you do when you love someone? You learn their favorite everything, spend quality time with them, dole out words of affirmation. You learn their wants; you learn their needs. You anticipate those wants, and you anticipate those needs.

You know their flaws, and you embrace those flaws. You might even love them because of those flaws.

I am learning to love myself.

––––––––––––

My eyes stare back at me, judging me, watching me from the mirror on the wall. I return the gaze, staring back at myself. I hear the words whispered in my head: I am enough. I am whole. I am me.

I am a sister, girlfriend, daughter, friend. I am a writer, actor, teacher. I am that and so much more.

––––––––––––

I am an extrovert. I love being around people, and I find joy in the laughter shared with others. I used to be one hundred percent extrovert. Then ninety-eight percent extrovert, two percent introvert. Then ninety, ten. Eighty-five, fifteen.

I'm finding the balance between spending time with others and spending time with myself. Recharging my batteries has become a form of self-care that I take very seriously. I recognize when I'm running on low battery, when I've put my body into overdrive and need to take a step back because driving on autopilot is more about existing than really, truly living.

Sometimes taking time for myself means finding joy in alone time. Sometimes that means I miss out on things, gatherings, activities, events. Sometimes that means I have to say no.

———————

It was not easy the first time I said no. I said no to hanging out because I was tired of being strung around. I said no to hanging out because I had been so busy and just needed to slow down. I said no to hanging out because my body was hurting, telling me that now was not one of those times that I push it to or beyond its limits.

It was not easy the second time I said no, and it wasn't easy the third, or fourth, or fifth. It's not always easy, but sometimes it is easier than it was before.

Standing up for myself sometimes simply means taking care of myself. It means listening to my body. It means realizing that people are flawed—I am flawed—but sometimes their flaws exist in a way that hurts me or disrespects me. It's a testament of love to myself when I choose to let go, and it's a testament of love to myself when I find the courage to say no.

———————

I had to say no this time, maybe next time as well. I am protecting myself, I tell myself. I know myself, I tell myself. This is a trigger for me, I tell myself.

I have spoken my truth, sought understanding, patience, and compassion while cutting open my soul and sitting vulnerable on the couch, in person, over the phone.

I have been judged, misjudged, and I know what is in store if I don't say no. And so I say no. This time. Maybe next time as well.

To protect myself. Because I know myself. And this is a trigger for me.

Digging deep enough to learn, know, understand, accept, and predict my triggers takes a great deal of thinking and analyzing. Not only do I know what triggers me and when I am triggered, but I have also uncovered the reasoning behind the triggers. I might be flawed for having these triggers, or it might just be part of being human. But I worked past recognizing these flaws so that I could find compassion for myself.

I know certain loud sounds bring me back to those thirty-six hours of sleepless torture. I know certain situations make me feel trapped, like I was, like I felt, more than once before. I know certain conversations, movies, and news will make me emotional because I feel empathy so deeply.

I now honor my flaws in a way that is respectful to myself.

I am ashamed. I hide behind the truth so well that even I cannot see it, simply don't understand it. I am nothing if not ashamed.

I am apologetic. I dole out a cacophony of unwarranted sorries, apologizing for a trait I see as my biggest flaw, for something I cannot control.

So I take control. I stop feeling ashamed and I stop apologizing.

Just as courage is defined not by a lack of fear but the ability to overcome it, resilience is built not by completing easy tasks but by conquering the challenging ones.

They call me resilient but I feel like I am dying inside. I feel like I am dying inside but I pick myself up from the puddle of my tears, stand atop the pile of granola bar wrappers, put on a shirt with such deliberate, measured movements it must be my first time getting dressed, and I step on the bus with energy I muster only from willpower.

I am told I am resilient until I believe and see that I am, in fact, resilient. I am taking control of my own life, and I am beginning to find happiness again.

———————

I am talking about what happiness is, what it means, how it can most accurately and best be defined. I am sharing my thoughts with a friend who asked, and suddenly we are poking holes in a manifestation. We brainstorm a myriad of answers until we have only one.

It is a casual yet intentional conversation. It is meaningful and has us wondering if the feeling of happiness is universal, if the root cause is the same across the globe.

We consult the dictionary. We consult our past experiences, our distant and recent joyful, pleasurable, and euphoric moments. We come up with our own muddled definition, left open-ended with the potential to be ever-changing.

———————

I am ever-changing, ever-evolving, sometimes skipping, sometimes strolling, sometimes dragging my feet down the path toward becoming a better version of my younger self.

I am seeking success, defining it, navigating what success is, what it means to me, and in the process, I encounter my greatest achievement.

———————

I believe in myself. It is the most difficult thing I've ever done. I am choosing to direct my own path. I am taking risks—great risks—without anyone holding my hand. I know my value, my worth. I know that I am not a burden, and I try to remind myself of that when I think about asking for help.

I believe in myself even though I have failed, will fail,

might fail. I believe in myself enough to take the plunge because I know, if I fall, if I fail, I'll make it through to the other side, even when hopelessness and helplessness are knocking on the door.

Rejection cuts with a sharp, jagged knife leaving behind a scar that stands out from the others. Standing out from the rest is just what I needed to avoid rejection, but instead I blend into the crowd of wannabes, dreamers, risk-takers, artists, and lovers.

Rejection, I see now, is an opportunity, and so I choose to believe in myself. And so I will make an opportunity for myself. I will make many opportunities for myself. I will dream, and then do, and then dream, and then do.

I am watching the sunset, and tomorrow I will watch the sunrise. I breathe in, breathe out, breathe in, breathe out. I am calm. I am dreaming. I am patient. I am hopeful.

I watch the colors change, mix, brighten, and then fade. I rest my hand over my heart and see that it, too, will change, will brighten, will fade.

I am calm. I am dreaming. I am patient. I am hopeful.

Patience with others comes easier than patience with myself. I see the same struggle with eager students. I see myself— younger, older—in them.

I lean down and whisper words of encouragement, remind them that mistakes are just their tiny brains growing so that they can learn, tell them that they have to make mistakes to learn, show them how even I—someone older, someone wiser—make mistakes still.

My brain is growing, and it is learning how to be patient with myself.

A difficult conversation needs to happen, is currently happening. I am learning when to listen and when to advise, and I am learning when to ask for listening and when to ask for advice.

I am learning how to communicate, how to be a good communicator. My natural instinct—the human natural instinct in uncomfortable social situations—is to fix things. Sometimes that leads to walking away, ignoring or avoiding confrontation. Sometimes that results in offering advice where no advice is wanted or maybe even needed. I am learning to communicate without charge.

I am incredibly vulnerable right now. I've just spilled the beans, a giant, whopping can of them, into the speaker on my cell phone, and I am waiting patiently for a response on the other end.

I know what I want to hear, and I have an idea of what I might hear. I think what I will hear will not be what I want to hear. I think what I will hear will be what I need to hear but not now, not what I need at this moment in time. Right now I just need to be heard. I just need to be listened to.

And so I ask for listening—only listening. Let me spill my beans, I say, and let me spill them some more. Let me unveil my hidden pain and speak, unfettered, about what and how I'm feeling, about what and how I've changed—will change, might change.

I lose track of what I'm talking about. I don't know in what direction my rambling speech is going and so I steer left, steer right, steer left right left right right right left.

Suddenly, I'm talking about how I, you, we have so much—so, so much—to learn.

I write about what I've learned, am learning, want to learn, hope to learn.

I write what I learned about love while traveling solo through the mountains and jungle and desert and city of Peru. I write about what I learned from a class of preschoolers with special needs. I write a summary of what I've learned through three decades on this earth, and what I learned when I traded in the island life for the city life. I write about learning to actually be open-minded instead of just thinking I am open-minded.

I write about time, about learning how to forgive the unforgivable because that's what it takes to free myself and move on. I write about healing, and how I learned that time doesn't heal all wounds. I write about learning that it isn't my fault, was never my fault.

I write about the invisible backpack that collected stones and weighed me down, and I write about unloading those stones one at a time until that invisible backpack was empty.

I write about authenticity and I write authentically.

I write a letter of love to my someday child. I write about honesty and I write honestly. I implore my child to be curious and ask questions, and I tell my child that I will always answer truthfully. I tell them that, yes, I have run away from my problems and, no, it did not solve anything. I tell them that, yes, some people have more things—bigger things—than us, but no one has an imagination like you, my child.

I tell them what it means to follow their dreams. I tell them that I hope they grow up to be embarrassed about nothing and genuine about everything.

I tell them what it means to look different but be the same, or look the same but be different. I tell them that, yes, I have harbored hate in my heart and it tore me apart but that, no, I don't have that hate anymore. Because I wanted to bring them into a world full of love and I could not do that with hate in my heart.

I tell my child that sometimes they will get lost or be lost, that sometimes they will feel afraid or judged or forgotten. I tell them that they must love harder and love more to make those feelings go away.

I tell my child that the feeling of being loved is something you can't write in the stars, but that there is another feeling, a greater feeling, of having someone to love—like you, my child. I tell them that loving is the greatest feeling—and the greatest gift—in the world.

I tell them that the best gift you can give me, my child, is the gift of loving not me, but yourself.

THE SOLDIER'S CHOICE
J.W. Capek

The black and white news reels at the movie theatre were dominated by the Nazi war machine crashing through countries and demolishing populations. A picture clip of the man with a small mustache screaming in German to multitudes of soldiers loomed over the audience. Seeing the images on the large screen made the dangers feel real even within the safety of the mid-western plains. The evacuation of Dunkirk had foretold England's collapse. The ominous warnings were all there. Another worldwide war threatened to include America as dictators in Germany, Italy, and Japan united in purpose of world domination.

In the Autumn of 1940, a party of young adults enjoyed a picnic on the Rock River, Illinois, and William met Ella. William had a slim face and stature, always wore his glasses, and sometimes looked more serious than he really was. Three years from high school graduation, operating a Cross Saw at the Sash and Door with his father and uncles, and spending time with friends filled his life until now.

Ella was visiting her married sister and mutual friends

had brought her to the gathering. Where William was quiet and reserved, looking at the world through his glasses, he saw Ella to be vibrant and spontaneous in making new friends. Her greeting smile at William was warm and sincere and throughout the evening he admired her friendly approach to everyone. Her blond pageboy kept breaking into curls as she laughed or tossed her head sitting around the bonfire on the riverbank. When the blaze wore down and couples began pairing off out to the darkness, Ella remained near the fire pit with a cadre of people and William was pleased to be included. Mostly, he just listened. They talked of work, of fun experiences, and of course, the Conscription of young men.

"Well, he signed it! FDR signed the Conscription Act, so we'll be in this war soon enough," one young man, Toby, said as he roughly stoked the coals.

"We don't know that," said his friend. "The President was just doing it as a cautionary measure."

"Sure, Sure, just like the last war. We'll be 'Over There' any time now," Toby said tensely.

"What does it really mean?" asked Ella. She seemed uneasy with the war talk and she shivered in spite of the fire.

Toby's friend answered her, "It means all our lives are going to change one way or another. Whatever plans we had, what plans we make in the future will all be influenced by someone else's war." He looked at the fire and sighed, "Maybe it won't come to war."

"Yeah, like that's going to happen," Toby said bitterly. "The news reels, the papers, even the radio shows all talk about it happening sooner or later." He stabbed his stick into the flames.

"But, it's so far away. Why can't we just stay out of it?" Ella asked, trying to find some explanation. Looking around the friends at the fire, she added, "I can't imagine any of you going to battle." She moved closer to William who remained quiet but took her hand.

After the picnic, William saw Ella with other friends

until they were seriously dating by winter and into the spring. With his quiet manner, he always listened to her intently as she would chatter away. He did not dwell on the changes affecting them all and the premonitions of war. He was a good friend and his open admiration made her feel beautiful. It was still a surprise that summer when he slipped a ring onto her left finger as they sat in a darkened theatre watching a movie with Clark Gable. Ella touched the ring. She started to speak, but she couldn't say anything without disturbing the quiet audience. Ella pulled her hand from his and twirled the ring on her hand without being able to see it in the dark.

Leaving the theatre for a stop at the ice cream parlor, Ella glanced at the ring and her expression became one of immediate relief.

"Oh, William, it's my birthstone!" She smiled up at William. "I was afraid—I mean—I thought it was…"

Stopping to turn her towards him, William asked cautiously, "Don't you like it?" He held her other hand.

Ella admired the ring in the light from a street lamp. "William, it's beautiful, I've always wanted my birthstone! Thank you so much, but… I'm not sure what this means." Her smile was guarded.

William took both her hands in his and guided her to a street bench. With strolling lovers walking by, and potted trees, the bench was almost park-like in its setting.

"It means whatever *you* want it to mean, Ella." William hesitated, gathered his courage and said, "I love you, Ella." Those were the hardest words he had ever spoken. He rushed on, "I want to be your friend, your boyfriend, someone you can love… I hope, someone you can… marry." He smiled anxiously and pushed his glasses firmly on his nose.

Nervously, Ella took a breath and paused. Her hands fidgeted with her collar button. "Oh, William, I don't know how to answer you." A light, high pitched laughter accompanied her words.

William just looked at her expectantly and then she

looked directly at him to say, "Yes, you are my friend, a boyfriend for sure, but there's no way, I mean, I just don't love you the way..." Ella stopped, then glanced down. For once she seemed at a loss for words. "William, I do not want to hurt you. You are very dear to me. I just never thought of marrying you. We are both so young and just starting life and the future is very tenuous. Please, William," she said finally. "Can't we just be friends for now? Who knows what is coming, let's give it some time." She started to remove the ring.

William's smile faded, with an emptiness in the pit of his stomach, he said, "No, don't take it off, it looks perfect on your hand. Maybe with time..." He didn't finish. He tried not to look disappointed as he cleared his throat. With a darting look about them, he stood quickly and changed the subject. "Yes, yes, sounds like time for a hot fudge sundae" and he ushered her towards the parlor, lights and people where further talk would be impossible.

It was time now. William had enlisted at summer's end. William's parents had a going-away party for him and Ella attended. They promised each other to write but neither could vouch for their feelings in those letters. William looked at her with such longing, she gave him a quick kiss on the cheek, then turned to another friend.

After the party, William made a last stop at the cemetery and rested his hand on the family anvil. He remembered being a little towheaded boy holding his mother's hand when he first visited the family plot. The Blacksmith Anvil was a huge memorial of iron and stone in the Midwestern Cemetery. Then, he had to look up to the powerful metal mounted on a stone pedestal tombstone surrounded by the smaller stones.

To William Schmidt—the tall and lanky grown man now looking down on the monument—it remained a formidable reminder of his family's place among the living as well as those surrounding the anvil at rest. In the summer heat, the metal was warm to his touch. His family had immigrated from Germany, he remembered his grandfather who spoke with a strong accent. They left Europe to find a better life for all of them and brought the blacksmith skills with them. He loved the family heritage, but he loved America more. He wasn't waiting for the draft. He could only hope Ella might wait for him. It was the summer of 1941, and at age 21, William Schmidt was on his way to the Basic Training in the US Army.

William was conscientious and exemplary as an Army recruit. He didn't find the military to be much harder than his previous work at the lumber mill or the laboring jobs he held while in high school. His parents had weathered the Great Depression and passed its tough lessons onto William. Frugality, sacrifice, and labor weren't considered to be virtues, they were a necessity of life. Having enlisted early, William was with the other recruits at Camp Roberts, California, as they listened to the radio report about the attack on Pearl Harbor. President Roosevelt seemed to speak to each man personally about the "Day that will live in infamy." Now it was official, the United States was at war!

William was through Basic Training when the sergeant asked, "Who can drive a truck?" It may have been one of the few falsehoods of his life when Private Schmidt called out "I can, sir!" Although William had never driven a truck in his life, he was confident that he *could*. If he could operate a cross saw without losing any fingers, he thought driving a truck would be easy. He was also pragmatic. From the newsreels and articles in the newspaper, he figured it would be a long war ahead of him. Basic training and hours of marching gave him insight—he didn't want to walk through Europe. So, he didn't walk. He drove.

William was shipped to Fort Lewis in Washington State for winter training with the Truck Battalion. He approached the behemoth vehicle with the hesitancy of a bridegroom. Delivery or transport trucks he was used to at home were nothing like this mammoth. The CCKW or Deuce and a Half gave him a totally new perspective. There was a special scent to the cab: a mixture of wet canvas, metal, paint, fuel, mildewed leather. The mixture could be described as "military" and one that would become familiar for years. With his hands on the large steering wheel, he was "Bill, the driver." The heavy tactical vehicle with 6 axles and heavyweight tires could carry tons of cargo in any weather. He was trained to manage the enormous vehicle in terrain of mud or roads, mountains and snow covered passes. Chains had to be installed or removed and tires changed when flat.

Traveling in convoys, Bill would handle cargo, transport injured, and haul troops. The oversized truck had to be maneuvered on and off landing craft, up and down beaches and across fragile bridges. It was known as a 6X6 and became a mainstay of the Third Army, Third Infantry Division, through invasions and campaigns. For the following years, the all wheel drive 6X6 would be Bill's home, his work, his protection, his transportation through the horrendous conflict now known as World War Two.

In basic training and at Fort Lewis, mail was fairly steady. There were many briefings on what not to write to family. It was forbidden to name locations or duties or even fellow recruits other than their nicknames. Pearl Harbor was the catalyst of a full war effort and was impetus to following directions.

Ella's letters were chatty extensions of her packaging job at a meat packing plant. She would comment on changing styles of hair and clothing. News of friends was shared.

"Dear William, (I'm not used to calling you Bill.)
Remember Toby from the picnic? His draft number came up and he's deciding what to do. It seems strange for so many young men who seem to vanish overnight. When they return, they look wonderful in uniforms. We're

all still waiting to see what is coming. Where are you? What are you doing? Sincerely, Ella."

Bill's answers were brief and full of avoidance. He followed the rules and screened any answers to her questions. He knew officers would review the letters being sent out, so he was hesitant. He wished she could see him in action with his 6X6, he wished he could tell her about the guys he worked with and the strenuous days of training. For once, he had a lot to say but was restricted.

"Dear Ella,
The food's okay here, and plenty of it, although not like home. There's a lot of rain here but we can handle it. I know my letters might seem pretty short, but we're always busy without a lot of time to write. Of course, we're careful what we say. Goodnight, now, with greatest affection, Bill."

"Dear Bill,
I'm still getting used to your nickname. I have to write about something I've noticed. Since we got into this war, everybody's attitudes seem to have changed. People who were grouching over everything before are now doing whatever they can for the war effort. We have limits imposed on what we can buy but people are willing to sacrifice. Guys like you were considered crazy for enlisting early, now you are heroes. I hope I'll get to see you before you make any major moves. I saw your folks the other day and they sure like to get letters, too.
There are some guys our age working at the Meat Packing Company especially in the

salting department. We date sometimes while they wait for their draft numbers to come up. Do you have Dances for the military there? Here, there are service organizations starting to form to support our people in uniform. They are a lot of fun. Sincerely, Ella."

"Dear Ella,
I will be on furlough at home this Fall. I can't say where I'll be going next but my training seems to be complete. Please save time for me as my thoughts and affection are always with you. Bill."

The furlough was the last time Bill would see his family and Ella until after the war. No mention was made of his previous proposal and Ella always seemed to have friends about her. She was more lovely than ever and very animated. She would take Bill's arm and complement him on his uniform, asking questions about his merit badges and insignia. She mentioned dating others but gave no details. He couldn't seem to find a serious moment alone with her.

Too quickly, the leave was over and Bill was on a train to the rest of his life. The family saw him off, wondering when or if they'd see him again. Watching a child leave in uniform was a painful experience repeated over and over in stations across the country.

The first American troops landed in Algeria-French Morocco and marked the beginning of long and arduous campaigns for the Third Army: Tunisian, Sicilian, Naples-Foggia, Rome-Arno, Southern France, Rhineland, and Central Europe. Usually dragging a field cannon behind the truck, Bill hauled troops, injured, ammunitions and supplies and even German POW's. Friends, people, trains, ships, and trucks kept going… going… going.

Mail was sporadic for the troops in the European

theatre. On some campaigns the Army was moving so quickly, the mail couldn't keep up with them. Other times a bonus of letters would arrive. Bill noticed Ella's letters became fewer and fewer.

The campaign through North Africa was full of surprises for Bill. Raised in the Midwest, the desert was totally foreign. Water was the supreme goal for man, beast, and water-cooled engines. He had never seen so much sand nor experienced sandstorms. Gritty sand would seep through every crack and even the wrinkles in a soldier's body. Filters had to be cleaned, water jackets refilled, and the stares of local people ignored. He found himself reminiscing about training in the snow. It would be a refreshing daydream while sweating in the heat. The unshaded metal on the 6X6 would be burning to touch, and gloves only made quick repairs possible. Canvas coverings were stretched over the support ribs on the bed to shade the troops who were lucky enough to hitch a ride. Bill knew he made the right choice when he said he could drive a truck!

The poverty of the area was also new to Bill in spite of the Depression he'd seen firsthand. Destitute people begged the soldiers for whatever they could spare. Hands reached out to the soldiers. Some had trinkets to sell and Bill bought a leather patch bag to send his mother and some traditional shoes for his sister. He really didn't think the gifts were appropriate but wanted his family to know he was thinking of them in a far and exotic country. It was a kind way to give money to the poor people drawn to the troops.

There was a saying in Bill's family, "I cried because I had no shoes until I saw the man who had no feet." In North Africa and for the rest of the war experience, the adage was a reality to Bill. In one dusty village, the beggars were almost blocking his way when Bill saw the man with no feet. He stumbled along with the others on his two scarred stumps. His feet had been cut off, unevenly, and he only had the ragged edges of a cloak to wear. Two gnarled sticks were used as canes. Bill made sure he got a few coins and always remembered him. No matter how difficult events became, there was *always* someone worse off. Witnessing such poverty and desperation, he felt blessed with the 6X6 and rarely complained. He knew if he did gripe about Army life, the man with no feet would be there to remind him of his blessings.

Tunisia, Sicily, Naples and finally, Rome-Arno. It was hard to believe when the Third Army convoy drove through Rome. All of the pictures from schoolbooks showed the Coliseum and here he was! Bill was driving around the Roman Coliseum. There was a pause in the campaigns with a stabilizing in Rome. With a day off duty, Bill and friends went to St. Peter's Basilica. Bill thought it would be special to send a card to Ella because she was a devout Catholic. He had not heard from her recently, but thought the mail was just fouled up. He wanted her to know he was thinking of her even if he could only send it through APO mail.

The breathtaking beauty of the dome and artwork made Bill just stand in awe. He only wished he could share it with Ella. He was disappointed in the sales tables and vendors actually selling inside the magnificent church. Then again, he thought, there was a war on and he was just visiting, but the image lingered with the scent of incense and candles.

Bill was in Southern France when he received a "Dear John Letter." He read it in the cab. He'd seen others get such notes, usually claiming how sorry the correspondent was to write. Ella had met a man at work, they had fallen in love, and were married before his enrollment in Officer Cadet training. He was going to be a pilot and she would travel with him while he was in training. Ella completed the letter hoping she and Bill could remain "good friends."

Bill had never wanted to be "good friends" with Ella. Worst of all, she was marrying a fly boy, an officer in the Army Air Corps, while Bill was a ground pounder driving a truck! Dropping the letter, he beat his fist into the dashboard. He just wanted to love her and now she was gone. The guys in the platoon left him alone in his cab. There wasn't much they could say to another "Dear John." There was, however, something they could do!

The soldiers in back of the truck "liberated" a case of French wine from an abandoned winery. It was a perfect opportunity to get totally drunk and Bill didn't need coaxing! After the night's indulgence, Bill the driver, awoke in his cab to find he was surrounded by thick woods. The CCKW was parked behind huge trees. His head hurt and he couldn't remember how he got there but the rest of the guys were gradually waking up and getting out of the truck to look at the surroundings in amazement.

"Where are we?" one private asked. Everyone looked to Bill.

"I don't know!" Bill was incredulous. "Where's the corporal? Who has a map?"

"Where is everybody?"

"Oh, shit, how did we get here?"

"We better get back before we're AWOL!"

Bill looked at the blocked truck and at its two flat tires. He was dubious about their next action. "We can't leave until the tires are changed," and he gestured for help. The men started milling about trying to find the tools needed. Occasionally, one would stop to vomit.

"Bill" A Private said. "I hate to tell you, but your two spare tires are flat, too"

"Oh shit!" called the Corporal. "You mean somewhere last night you changed two tires in the dark and then proceeded to run the others flat? How drunk were you?"

"Not as drunk as you, Corporal, because I was able to back this damn truck into this damn forest! Corporal!" Bill answered, although he still was questioning his own ability at this amazing feat.

By now, all the men were anxious so they quickly followed directions to repair the spare tires and swap them.

Getting out of the trees meant cutting down the ones blocking the way, and a few privates started sawing on them. The scent of cut wood reminded Bill of his work at the mill. With careful maneuvering, Bill was able to follow yelled directions and drive slowly. He flinched at the sounds of fresh wood splintering as he scraped by it. He exited the woods towards a near road. It was already crowded with their company, moving out. The platoon loaded into the truck, Bill slipped into a convoy space and left the forest behind.

Bill never included this episode in his letters. He didn't tell his parents of his fears when German aircraft would strafe the trucks lined up on a road. One strafing caused him to leap from the CCKW to land on a shoulder beside the road with his back end up in the air. He could only think of the Army informing his mother that he died getting shot in the butt. He never wrote what it meant to race through the night to get wounded to the aid station, only to arrive too late. After the war, there would be time to tell stories. Or not. First, a soldier had to get home after the war.

In Germany near the end of the war, there were still the overhead sounds of Army Air Corps on their way to bomb the remaining German war machine into submission. The roar of the engines was unmistakable as was the sound of flak. Too often there followed the warning wail of impending crash and explosion of aircraft. The infantry could appreciate the work of the Air Corps as they saw the pounding it had given the Nazi war machine. It eased their advances into the center of Germany. They also recognized the cost in American flyer lives.

The convoy on the ground now moved quickly through liberated towns, often accompanied by cheers and words of appreciation. Bill was stopped in a convoy line in one German village when an old man stared at the big 6X6 and approached it. Bill tensed, not knowing what the man was planning. The German reminded him of his grandfather in another time on a different continent. The old gentleman reached out and patted the fender with a look of admiration. He looked up at Bill behind the steering wheel and said "Das ist ein guter Wagen." His hand stroked the curve of metal and he repeated "Guter Wagen."

Bill smiled, tipped his helmet and agreed, "Ja guter Wagen!" It was a good truck! The 6X6 ahead started moving and the procession lumbered out of the village but Bill would always recall a German Grandfather who appreciated the industry of America. Guter Wagen.

The war was moving rapidly with both the Americans and Russians attempting to claim territories. A letter from Bill's mother hoped for a quick end so her son could come home. There was a P.S. to the letter saying, "I've heard that Ella's husband is Missing In Action. I have no details."

Victory in Europe, V-E Day, May 8, 1945, was a boisterous celebration by all the troops in Europe. Bill was in the German heartland and saw the elation in the all the soldiers and German people as well. Everyone was ecstatic the war was over no matter which side you were on. World War Two was over! In the enthusiasm of victory, the lingering effects of the war could be ignored—the devastation of whole populations, the tortures of the concentration camps, the monumental loss of lives and social disruption. For V-E day there was merriment and carnival!

It was not over for the Asian Theatre. The hardened combat troops in Europe were destined to be shipped to Asia. An even longer war was anticipated as islands were sorely bought with Allied lives. The casualties anticipated in a military campaign against the Main island of Japan horrified the decision makers.

Bill's unit was being prepared to ship home on furlough before being sent to Japan.

On August 6 and 9, 1945 the only two atomic bombs ever used during warfare ended the war completely. On V-J Day, Victory in Japan, August 14, 1945 the exhilaration exploded!

It was over.

All Over.

The men and women who survived were part of a generation of pride. For the men and women who did not return, they were revered by all veterans. After four years in service and 2 ½ of them driving through war torn countries, Bill was honorably discharged. Years later when asked if he would like to take a tour of Europe, Bill answered, "Been there. Have no desire to go back."

Returning to the Midwest and to work at the local Sash and Door, Bill asked friends about Ella. He had heard she was waiting for her husband's return since March. His plane went down just weeks before the end of the war in Europe. No one knew anything more.

When Bill and Ella did meet again, at the ice cream parlor, she was as beautiful as he remembered. Genuinely happy to see him, she rushed into his arms and hugged him tightly. Being discharged, he was in civilian clothes. Ella couldn't seem to let go. After a long moment she stepped back to look at him but kept holding his hand. His maturity was obvious in his expression and solid musculature. He still wore glasses on his slim face. Her smile was for him but now there was a touch of sadness brimming in her eyes.

"Oh, Ella, I am so sorry to hear about your husband being missing," Bill said sincerely. "You know it's still a mess over there. He'll probably show up at some camp with his crew. It happens all the time. Guys just walk into the nearest post and the paperwork keeps them in limbo. The only reason I'm home so quickly, was so I could be shipped to Japan."

"Bill, it's been so long since we've heard anything!" Ella didn't try to hold back her tears. "We—the other crew families—are in constant touch. We keep writing the government and each other. My brother-in-law is in the Red Cross and he is constantly searching records and files." Once again she reached out to him and he held her until the tears wore her out. Bill walked her over to the same bench where he had proposed so long ago and waited quietly until she was ready to talk.

"Where are you staying now?" Bill asked.

"I'm at my mother's, but it's very hard there. Did you know my father died?"

"No, I hadn't heard. Again, I am so sorry."

"He died shortly after the baby was born and we heard... Franklin, my husband..."she paused and took a deep breath. "My older sister is there with her two little girls, she has no where else to go. The little girls are so fond of Stacy, they play and help take care of the baby." She tried to smile thinking of her nieces.

"Stacy?"

Ella nodded. "Bill, I'm a mother now. Stacy was born in March and just two weeks later, her Daddy was listed as Missing." Her expression was pained.

"Did her father get to know about her?"

"Yes." She nodded hurriedly with tears again threatening. "We got a telegram to him and he was so glad she was a little girl. He always hoped for a little girl. She'll be waiting for him when he comes home. We all will." She dabbed her eyes with a handkerchief.

Because of her anguish, Bill tried to change the subject, but she appeared to want to talk. He watched her with his own agony because there was very little he could do.

"I had been dreaming of Franklin so often," Ella began. "I was always trying to catch him, to talk to him. One night, I'd had a dream where he stopped running away and turned to say, 'I have something to tell you.' Then I woke up. The next morning, I wrote my daily letter to Franklin, fed Stacy, and started the laundry chores. I was at home hanging up diapers in the side yard when the telegram came. His letters had stopped but that was often the case with mail hold ups. The telegraph boy wouldn't look me in the eye, he just came around the gate to get my signature. I signed and slipped the brown envelope into my pocket with the letter I was going to take to the mailbox as soon as the laundry was finished. One diaper after another. Then they were all hanging in the sun and I couldn't avoid the telegram any longer. I took it out and read:

April 17, 1945

THE SECRETARY OF WAR DESIRES ME TO EXPRESS HIS DEEP REGRET THAT YOUR HUSBAND HAS BEEN MISSING IN ACTION OVER GERMANY SINCE 31 MARCH 1945. IF FURTHER DETAILS OR OTHER INFORMATION ARE RECEIVED YOU WILL BE PROMPTLY NOTIFIED.

THE ADJUTANT GENERAL
US ARMY

Ella looked up at Bill for a silent moment then added. "I never did mail the letter in my pocket, I just put it away."

Bill could say nothing because of the tightness in his throat. He knew how often her story was repeated to families throughout the country. He had written letters of condolences to some of them. Just as a friend of their son, he wanted them to know they weren't alone.

Neither Bill or Ella were the same people from four years ago but they fell into a pattern of close friendship. They spent more time together and Bill would carry the baby. It felt so good to him to hold a healthy, well fed baby after some of the children he had seen in war. Stacy had the scent of clean baby powder and washed clothes and would cuddle into his arms as the two adults walked along at the park or were running errands. With the tension in her home, Ella preferred to spend her waiting time with his friendship. Bill never went into details about his own experiences, he just listened to her talk about following her husband around the country for Pilot training before his deployment. She and Franklin would grasp whatever time they could find to be together.

Bill just listened, and it comforted her the most.

Bill was at Ella's front door when she met him with an expressionless face. There was no emotion, only a dead stare on her face. She said nothing, just handed him the telegram, and he read to himself.

October 18, 1945

THE SECRETARY OF WAR HAS ASKED ME TO EXPRESS HIS DEEP REGRET THAT YOUR HUSBAND WAS KILLED IN ACTION OVER GERMANY 31 MARCH 1945. HE WAS PREVIOUSLY REPORTED MISSING IN ACTION. I REGRET THAT OFFICIAL REPORT NOW RECEIVED ESTABLISHES DEATH. CONFIRMING LETTER FOLLOWS.

THE ACTING ADJUTANT GENERAL
US ARMY

Bill took Ella in his arms, rocked her gently. As she wept, he made a decision. He loved her as he always had from the first night by the firelight of the beach party. Coming home meant being with Ella. The scent of her hair was a delicious memory. If a world war could not separate them, it was right for them to be together now. He would act upon his decision when they both were ready.

Again, time and friendship allowed Ella to grieve, and Bill to re-enter a civilian world.

Veterans from war have a true reverence for those who do not return. With such respect for Franklin, and love for Ella, Bill finally expressed his deepest feelings for her. Seated on a swing on Ella's front porch, Bill was as honest with himself as he was with her. He took her hand with the simple gold wedding band she still wore. "Ella" he began with confidence, "I know you can't love me the way you did Franklin, but I will be a good husband to you and good father to Stacy. We can make the future happen for us as a family. Please, say you will marry me." His eyes never left hers as he gently stroked her face.

Ella looked deeply into the eyes of a man who loved her, loved her child, and made a vow of commitment. Her hesitation was brief, then she removed the gold band and put it in her pocket. She reached out to the dearest man she knew. She said, "Yes, Bill. Yes!"

Forty years later, the flowers and candles at the funeral were overshadowed compared to the bold red and white stripes of the flag with its pristine stars on blue. It covered and adorned the casket. Beyond the windows, the winter was beginning with warning flakes of snow.

One lady in the chapel second pew whispered to her friend, "William Schmidt was such a pillar of the community, a lovely man. He died too early. His heart just gave out on him."

Stacy, the grown daughter sitting in family row turned and said gently, "His heart didn't 'give out.' He wore it out with love."

A DIFFERENT HOLIDAY
Amber Rainey

This isn't how I imagined my first *adult* Thanksgiving. I'd had everything so perfectly planned out, it could have been in a *Southern Living* magazine spread. Mom, Aaron, and I would all be in the kitchen cooking up a storm while Dad and Grandpa kicked back in the recliners in the living room, watching the Macy's Thanksgiving Day parade because it was too early for the Cowboys game. Aaron and I would both have our girlfriends over and they would be sitting in the barstools at the counter gossiping or just teasing us for the frilly aprons Mom insisted we wear, just to embarrass us in front of them. Everyone would be laughing and talking—having a great time and it would just feel right.

A few things from that dream are present today. I'm in the kitchen—but not with my *blood* family. My friend, Katie, and I are doing all the cooking and she is doing her best with winging it because none of the recipes I want to serve are written down—they are all in my head because they are family recipes that have been verbally passed down through generations of my family. I spent years helping Mom in the kitchen and perfecting those recipes. Katie is a great sport though and she really listens when I tell her each step. I don't think I could have completed this meal without her.

We don't have recliners, *yet*. Thomas thought they were too ancient for a modern living room so we only have an odd modular couch thing. A couple of our friends are chatting on them—tacitly ignoring the parade that I insisted must be on. Thomas rolled his eyes good-naturedly and indulged me. He knows how much this day means to me and he is doing his best to keep me happy. I still think he is going to flip his lid when I insist the Cowboys game be on, even while we are eating. He knows the *no electronics during dinner* rule but this is the Cowboys Thanksgiving game and it doesn't matter what time it airs—the television will be on that channel come hell or high water.

We are an odd mishmash of friends with nowhere else to go for Thanksgiving. Our families don't want us with them—some of us have been completely disowned while others of us could not stand to be with a family that doesn't really want us there. Amy is here because she is a black sheep in her family and she can't stand another Thanksgiving listening to her racist and bigoted relatives fighting over things that she is completely against. The six of us, me, Thomas, Amy, Katie, Grant, and Brad, are all happy with the lives we have chosen but each of us misses parts of our previous lives. We've formed our own family, bonded not by blood but by similar stories.

Katie and I are putting the finishing touches on the food when the doorbell rings. Thomas gives me a look and I shrug. We weren't expecting anyone else. We have a silent moment where we agree that we should both answer the door. The previous chatter has gone silent and this moment feels like it is important. I put the oven mitt down and walk over to the door and Thomas joins me. He opens the door and I swear the entire room behind me gasps. No one has ever met Aaron but they've seen his picture hanging prominently on the wall—the two of us smiling back—feeling like we ruled the world.

"Um… hi… Andrew," Aaron says bashfully, his girlfriend giving a small grin and wave.

"Aaron… why? What?" I sputter, looking around him as if the rest of my family is hiding in the bushes, ready to pop out.

He shakes his head. "It's just us. We can leave if you don't have enough."

"Nonsense, he's cooked enough food for an army," Thomas laughs and ushers Aaron and his girlfriend through the door.

I'm still gobsmacked and everyone can tell, their eyes darting back and forth between me and my brother. Thomas begins making introductions and I turn my back for a moment, trying to quell the tears I fell threatening to come. No, this is not like any Thanksgiving I have ever imagined but it just became even more perfect.

I grew up in the Piney Woods of East Texas. I was born into a very Southern family—the epitome of what most people think of when they talk about us. I would like to say that my family was different but unfortunately, we were probably exactly what people thought of us. My mother's family had been in Texas since before it was a republic. My father's family practically created the south—coming to the shores of Georgia long before the United States of America existed and spreading out from there across the South until they finally reached Texas in the last couple of centuries. Unfortunately, years and years of living in the South, coupled with the Civil War and the aftermath had left my family poor farmers. Sure, you could make a living off farming but it no longer made your rich. Drought years always seem to wipe out the times of plenty. My father had been smart enough to make some small investments here and there in his youth, so we at least had a house and some land that wasn't owned by the bank.

In East Texas, there is just about a church on every corner. Plenty of Christian denominations are represented but the one that wins out in terms of reach and membership is Southern Baptist. My family belongs to this denomination and it isn't for the faint of heart. You have to be incredibly devoted to God in order to belong. We went to Sunday School every Sunday morning, then worship service. Then we went back on Sunday evening for another worship service. On Wednesday evening, we were back at services again. If there was a revival, we went to the service every night of the revival, sometimes for two weeks straight. Vacation Bible School was a pillar of our summers. If there was a holiday, such as Easter or Christmas, we were back at special services. On top of that, we prayed at every meal and every sports game and whenever a need arose, at the whims of Mom and Dad.

The other culture of the south is food. Food is the lifeblood of everyone but it is an art in the South. Did you just have a baby? Here is a casserole. Are you sick or in the hospital? We'll bring a meal over to your family. Of course, birthdays and holidays and just a perfect summer day are all that is needed to spark a barbecue or cookout. Did you have a death in the family? Of course, every family in the neighborhood will keep your loved ones fed for at least the next month. Food is the answer to everything. I once heard someone ask a Southerner why they lived in the South when it got so hot and muggy. The reply was, *"Once you've tasted the food you will understand!"*

Our lives pretty much revolve around these things: God, food, and football. In Texas, football is *the most* important sport... ever. If you are in high school, you are at the football game on Friday nights. Usually, you are either in the band, a cheerleader, or a player. Of course, in the larger schools, one can just be a spectator, but I grew up in a small town in a small high school and my father expected me to play football. *"Andrew, it's a family tradition. I played, your grandad played, his dad played..."* I think I heard that lecture in the womb and my dad didn't even know the gender I would be yet. My brother, Aaron, once mentioned that he wanted to drop out of flag football because it was too hot for practice. I don't think he ever recovered from the stare my father gave him. Truly, if looks could kill, Aaron would be dead. Dad's boys would play football and there would be no discussion.

Aaron and I were pretty good sons. Every child has their moments but I feel like we were well-behaved, god-fearing, model sons. We made our parents proud, whether it was at church, at school, or helping out on the farm. We didn't go out drinking or partying. We didn't cruise the strip with girls in our cars and we definitely didn't spend any time alone with a girl in our rooms or elsewhere. We were just decent, young men.

At least, that was the image I projected. As I started to hit my teens, I started crying into my pillow some nights. I prayed so hard every night for God to give me the strength to be a good man. I was devout in my beliefs and I was torn in half when what I deemed impure thoughts would intrude on a perfectly good day. I was afraid to talk to anyone for fear that I would lose everything I had worked so hard for. I was afraid of the judgment and damnation I knew would follow the revelation. I began pushing Aaron away, once my best friend in the whole world, because I feared I would rub off on him. I tried my hardest to ignore half of myself.

During my freshman year of high school, a new girl came to school. Phoebe was beautiful. She had dark brown hair and green eyes with long natural lashes. The other girls were incredibly jealous the moment Phoebe set foot on our campus. I was immediately enthralled, along with every other boy in our class and even some of the upperclassmen. I lucked out and Phoebe said yes to me. To this day, I don't know why she picked me over everyone else. On the night of our first date, I was so nervous I had to change my undershirt three times. Dad gave me the usual lectures about respecting her and not staying out past curfew. I nodded along as if really listening but if you asked me ten minutes later what Dad said, I don't think I could have repeated it. Aaron teased me all the way to the front door.

To say Phoebe was perfect is an understatement. We dated all through high school and she was always charming and funny. I loved being around her and I can honestly say now, I loved her. At the time, I thought maybe I had been mistaken and I didn't know what love felt like. I've had time to reflect on that more and I do know that I loved her. I once thought of marrying her but I don't regret never asking her. People come in and out of our lives for a reason. I could never thank Phoebe enough for being my first love. Her love gave me the strength I needed to admit to myself who I am.

The first time I really struggled with myself was as a junior in high school. Phoebe and I were still dating. We spent all the time we could together. It was a lucky happenstance that she and I went to the same church. It meant, once I started driving, that she and I could ride to and from church meetings together. We could sit in the same pew. Occasionally, we could even hold hands while the preacher gave his sermon. It all depended on what dress she was wearing and if our hands could be hidden in her skirt. Or if it was hot, I could take my jacket off and drape it on my lap so that I could hold her hand underneath. We were never explicitly told we couldn't hold hands but we also did not want an adult to yell at us or think we might be doing something against the *Good Lord's* approval. Phoebe and I never ran out of things to say to each other. She was smart in a way I never thought I was and she would laugh at me when I called myself a dumb jock. She always believed in me and I should have believed in myself more because, while I wasn't an honor student, my grades were really pretty good.

Phoebe and I were hanging out at the Dairy Palace when the feelings I thought I had mastered came rushing back and nearly knocked the wind out of me. It was a perfect, sunny day and we were eating ice cream. I distinctly remember chomping down on Banana Pudding flavored ice cream—just like a frozen version of my Nana's—when I looked up and saw my classmate, Mark, step onto the patio. I don't know why but at that moment, he looked like the sexiest male alive. I winced, looking around to see if I had spoken allowed, but Phoebe just kept talking to Courtney and no one else seemed to be the wiser. I looked back at Mark and could hardly take my eyes off him as he walked over to us. I was embarrassingly aware of how hyper-aroused I was feeling and quickly excused myself to go to the restroom. Once there, I threw cold water on my face and tried to gather my wits. I closed my eyes and prayed right then and there that God would forgive my thoughts.

For months after that day, I could hardly be in the same room with Mark without having some kind of fantasy of being with him and holding his hand like I held Phoebe's. Each night I would pray for forgiveness. I would plead with God to make it all stop. I had the perfect girlfriend, I was a quarterback on the football team. I was liked in school and in the community. I couldn't be such an abomination. How could I like Phoebe **and** Mark? God was not providing answers and my school work was suffering because of the stress and lack of sleep. Mom and Dad were called in and the school counselor suggested therapy. I resisted with everything I had in me and Dad relented on the condition that I bring my grades back up. I agreed and did everything I could to spend more time with Phoebe and put Mark out of my head.

During senior year, things settled out. If I started having any thought about any other person who was not Phoebe, I quickly squashed them by thinking about my Nana in her underwear. It seemed to work pretty well and my grades stayed up. There is so much happening in the senior year anyway, I was kept busier than I had been. I accepted a football scholarship to the University of Texas. Phoebe was going to college on the east coast and we were going to be separated. I understand now what she meant about long-distance relationships but it broke my heart when she broke it off with me. I think she would have stayed if I had asked her but I'd spent so long conflicted about my feelings that I didn't want to weigh her down with my issues. We parted on good terms and she still sends me an occasional email.

College was exciting. Being a Longhorn was something I had hoped for since I was a little boy. Everything was going well when I met Thomas in my sophomore year. Thomas is a very good looking, smart, and friendly guy. I was studying on the bleachers one day before practice when Thomas sat down next to me and started talking a mile a minute. It was kind of endearing. By now, I had learned to temper my attraction to anyone not of the female species but I had to admit I felt a little zing when we shook hands. Thomas didn't hide who he was and he didn't censor what he said.

"So, I was wondering if you were free tomorrow night. For dinner?" he asked me.

I almost choked on my own spit. I can only imagine whatever look was on my face because his smile dimmed just a little bit but it didn't seem to deter him. He just sat a little taller and waited for my reply.

"I'm not... I don't... "

"Oh, you're not out?"

I shook my head slowly, still trying to comprehend where the conversation was going.

"I'm not gay. At least, I don't think I am... I like women. I had a girlfriend..."

"But?"

"But? There's no but... she left for college. We just split up because of the distance," I tried to explain.

"I see."

Thomas watched me for a moment and then looked out at the field. I could tell he was clearly thinking about something but couldn't put my finger on what might be going on in his head. He looked over at me and then pulled a pen and paper out of his bag, He quickly wrote down a note and handed it to me with a wink.

"Talk to you later."

He didn't wait for my response, just skipped down the bleachers and walked off across the field. I looked down at the note and saw he'd written his name and phone number with the message *Call me if you need answers... or for that dinner :)*

I held onto that note for a week. I prayed and prayed God would take the temptation from me but everywhere I turned, I thought I saw Thomas. His bright blue eyes and his midnight hair were haunting my dreams. I did everything I could to get him out of my head and when I couldn't, I finally called the number.

"Hello?"

"Um, hi... it's me."

"Hmm, and does *me* have a name?"

I took the phone from my ear and looked at it as if he could see me giving him the strange look. I nodded my head and rolled my eyes at myself.

"Andrew," I replied.

"Nice to meet you, Andrew. Now, I think you have questions and you've never had anyone to answer them."

"Well... yes?"

"So, dinner?"

I rolled my eyes again and chuckled. He was definitely persistent. I contemplated my answer for a long time while the silence rolled on. It felt like an eternity before I was finally able to brush off my fear of being a sinner and say yes. It was one dinner—I wasn't committing any sins by eating with a person.

I met Thomas at his off-campus apartment. We went out to the local pizza joint and just chatted about what I considered normal things—where we were from, our families, our studies. Nothing about my conflicted feelings about men or my horror at my own shortcomings. When we finished, Thomas invited me upstairs to his apartment. I fought the rising horror and the voice in my head telling me I was going to hell. The truth was, I felt more myself in Thomas' company than in my own. I agreed and we went upstairs. Thomas offered me a drink and I accepted. I sat awkwardly on his couch while he fetched the drink.

"You can relax, I'm not going to bite."

I jumped at the sudden intrusion to my thoughts. He laughed and that helped relax me a little as it gave me the chance to laugh at myself. He sat next to me and waited for me to speak. I got uncomfortable again and started bouncing my leg—a nervous trait I had picked up from Dad's side of the family. Thomas reached out and put a hand on me. The jolt of arousal sending my brain in a tailspin. I jumped back and Thomas jumped up.

"I'm so sorry to startle you," he apologized.

"No, no... I'm just not used to... I don't know what came over me," I stammered.

We both sat back down and my leg started bouncing again but this time I checked it and made it stop. I took a quick gulp of my drink and determined to ask him the real question swirling around in my brain since that day in the bleachers. I closed my eyes, took a huge breath in and then let it out.

"What's wrong with me?" I blurted.

Thomas laughed, "Come again?"

"What's wrong with me? I like women—they are beautiful—and yet..."

"You also like men?"

"Sometimes... not all of them... but some are... very attractive."

Thomas nodded. "You're bisexual."

"That's impossible. It goes against nature and God's plan."

"And yet, you are. It's natural, just not seen that way in certain religions."

I stood up and brushed a hand through my hair. I couldn't believe what he was telling me. It was just too much for me to process. I was devout in my faith and I followed God's teachings. Why was I being punished? Thomas got up and pulled a little folder out of a drawer. He handed it to me and I took it.

"This will help explain things. It has some resources for you. Once you've gotten some more answers, you know where I am. I would very much like to date you but only if you are ready."

"So, you are bisexual, too?"

Thomas shook his head, "Oh, no, I am as gay as they come but I think you are really attractive and I would like to get to know you better."

I left Thomas' apartment more confused than I had ever been. I took his folder and looked at all his resources. There was a number for a hotline and I called it and spoke to someone on the phone who walked me through what was happening and gave me a referral to a therapist that *"won't judge you."* I made an appointment to see the therapist and then several follow-up appointments after that one.

Eventually, Thomas and I began dating. I never told anyone in my family about him because I was too afraid of their judgment. I felt right with Thomas like I had felt with Phoebe. We just seemed to fit. He and I became closer and closer and by my senior year in college, we had become roommates and lovers and I had dreams of marrying him. The only problem was, the more I dreamed, the more the specter of my family's judgment loomed over me. It was Thanksgiving of that last year that I decided to invite Thomas to come home with me. He was overjoyed that he would be meeting my family and I was terrified. He tried to calm my nerves but nothing really helped.

Thomas got a usual Southern welcome from everyone. I hadn't told them he was my significant other. Mom still thought I was carrying a torch for Phoebe and just hadn't *found the right girl.* Thomas gave me a look over her head, which I tried to ignore but I am sure Aaron caught on to the tension long before it boiled over. I should have known staying at our house was going to amount to a disaster but I was so tense that I did not heed the warning signs.

We had stayed up late the night before playing games with my brother and his girlfriend. Thomas and I had argued a bit when we went to bed because Mom had made two separate beds. Thomas was angry that I still had not told them we were together and I kept begging for more time. Thomas had good reason to be upset. If I could not admit I loved him to my family, then our relationship was doomed. I couldn't see a way out of the problem. I wanted to console him and reassure him so we sat on my bed and ended up falling asleep. Mom, being the early bird, came in to wake me before the alarm and found us in bed together. That is when the poop hit the fan.

"Get out of my house, right now," she demanded, swatting at Thomas.

"What's going on in here?" Dad came rushing in.

"This filth was draping himself around Andrew. We don't allow faggots in our home. God is always watching!" Mom spewed her hatred at Thomas.

Thomas quickly got dressed, looking helplessly between my parents and me. Aaron came into the door frame and his eyes widened at the scene. Then, he turned around, ushering his girlfriend back down the hallway.

"Andrew, what is the meaning of this?" my father demanded.

I was frozen to the spot. Thomas was pleading with me with his eyes and my mother was staring daggers at him. She turned her gaze to me as if I was a hurt puppy and she had to protect me. It was that pitiful stare and the dejected expression coming across Thomas' features that gave me the courage for what happened next.

"Thomas and I are in love and I want to marry him," I replied, a little too loudly.

My mother's face drained of all color and my dad's

turned red. They looked at each other, then at Thomas, and finally at me. Suddenly, the realization of what I had said hit them and they both seemed to explode at the same time.

"Both of you out of my house, now!" Dad yelled.

"Damn you to hell, son. God will judge you," my mother added.

Thomas and I gathered what we could while my parents stared daggers at us. I let Thomas go out first and then I followed him into the hall. I gathered up our coats and was about to follow Thomas out of the house when my dad put an arm in front of me to stop me.

"Repent now, boy. If you walk out that door, you are dead to us," he warned.

I looked up and saw Aaron at the end of the hallway. I tried to beg for him to intervene but he just shook his head sadly and went into his room. My mom threw herself down on her knees and began praying for my soul and begging God for answers on where she went wrong. I looked out at Thomas in the driveway and then back at my father.

"Bye, Dad."

I was given a choice between the family of my birth or the love of my life. I chose the love of my life. I still love my mother and father, my grandparents, and my brother but I had to follow my heart. I had to give up a piece of myself in order to discover a new piece.

That disastrous Thanksgiving, we ate dinner at the local Waffle House before heading back to our apartment. Luckily, I had saved enough to finish paying off my senior year college dues because my father withdrew the final payment. Just after Christmas, I got a few boxes delivered by a moving company and a letter from my parents. They had sent me every last thing I owned at their house and informed me I was to never contact them again.

It had been two years since that Thanksgiving and this year, Thomas was determined not to let me mope through another holiday without my *traditions*. He'd arranged to have all the food I needed to cook our traditional holiday meal, as well as Katie to help me cook it. Thomas is a horrible cook. I think the man could burn water. He also asked our friends to come over so our table would not be laden with food and no one to eat it. He doesn't understand why I like a full house on the holidays but he knows it is just the *Southern* in me.

Thomas comes over and rouses me from my musings. I smile at him and he nods towards the kitchen, where Aaron and Katie have restarted the final preparations. He squeezes my shoulder and gathers our friends to start setting the table. I go into the kitchen and my brother tosses the oven mitt at me like old times. We settle into the routine fairly quickly and in no time at all, the table is laden with food. We have turkey, ham, sweet potatoes, dressing, green pea salad, green beans, rolls, gravy, pumpkin pie, pecan pie, and sweet potato pie. Thomas was right about having enough to feed an army. Thomas seats everyone, putting my brother at the opposite end of the table.

My brother smiles and winks at me, then rises and clears his throat. I groan and hope for the best. It was always my brother's fondest wish to embarrass me whenever he could and now I can only hope he is civil in whatever he says.

"Andrew, Sadie and I are very happy you welcomed us to this dinner. It hasn't been the same without you. I should have stood by you when Mom and Dad kicked you out of the family. I'm sorry about that and I'm sorry for the distance between us since then. I hope we can repair our brotherly bond. Thomas, I am looking forward to getting to know my brother-in-law. Here's to family!"

Everyone raises their glasses and clinks them together. Thomas grabs my hand under the table and squeezes and I am once again left feeling like I am about to cry. Someone asks about the marshmallows on top of the yams and Aaron launches into a diatribe on the merits of different toppings for the dish. Everyone else starts little conversations and Thomas leans over and gives me a peck on the cheek before grabbing some ham and passing it to Amy beside him.

I look around at my new family and parts of my original one and I feel a sense of peace for the first time in years. Learning I was bisexual and coming to grips with it may have changed some things but it didn't take away who I am as a person. I can still be the Southern gentleman with my culture of kindness and food and also be the loving husband to Thomas.

GIRL MEETS BOY
Angela Faro

Girl and Boy First Meet

It was the summer of '92. There were parties and bonfires and magic was in the air. It was a time in her life she would never forget. But more importantly, it was the summer she met him. Jason. He was handsome, charming, funny, and sweet. He was also a little wild, dangerous, and spontaneous. He was a bad boy and she was always a sucker for that.

Maria was new in town and she had only made a few friends so far. They were all a bit older than her—she normally didn't connect as well with people her own age. They didn't seem to get her, so people often were unkind to her. She was told many times she was an old soul by those who did get to know her. They were right too. For this was her fifth journey here on this earth. And it wasn't the first time her soul connected with his, nor would it be the last, but for today, we focus on this connection. This journey. This lifetime.

She was eighteen and just graduated high school. It was a hot August night and she was supposed to have been babysitting as far as her parents knew, she still lived at home so although she was an adult, she was expected to continue to follow their rules which did not allow for being out late at night. Instead she went with some friends to hang out at the Pilchuck bridge, a popular party spot that was on a secluded beach along the river. She had never been kissed, never drank any alcohol or done any illegal substances aside from smoking her cigarettes that made her feel so cool—silly as that may sound—ever since she was sixteen, and her new friends were set on corrupting her otherwise innocent mind. They would not succeed on this night, however.

They had managed to get their hands on a few cases of Schmidt Ice along with some weed, and magic mushrooms. There was plenty to go around since it was a small party, just a handful of friends. It would be a fun time for sure and certainly a memorable night in her life, one that she would cherish forever and be forever grateful that she stayed sober to remember it.

Maria was wearing her favorite little purple crop halter top and extra short cutoff jean shorts with simple flip-flops. She had never been very confident in her appearance because of how she had been treated by so many people growing up so she had no idea how beautiful she was. With an hourglass figure, bright blue eyes with thick eyelashes, full lips, long wavy sun-kissed auburn hair, soft and smooth skin with a peaches and cream complexion, and a charismatic personality to go along with it. Nevertheless she was oblivious.

Jason took interest in Maria right away when she arrived to the party with Jamie, Danielle, Andrea and Darneisha. He had his eye on her as the group approached, with an adorable smirky smile, his signature smile you could say. Maria simpered back at him shyly then her eyes quickly darted away only to continuously steal sidelong glances at him. He was so handsome in his blue jeans and a rock band t-shirt. Gorgeous sky blue eyes, long blonde hair... and he was six feet tall. He had a guitar and he was playing Silent Lucidity by Queensryche and seated next to him was his friend Alan. They had beer cans scattered all around and Alan was smoking pot using one of the empty beer cans to smoke it out of.

"Bummer, I should have brought my guitar," Maria lamented. She was also a guitar player and was still learning so this enticed her.

That she also played sparked Jason's attention even more. "What? You play? No way," he replied, interested.

Maria with a sheepish look said, "Well, I'm not anywhere near as good as you but I'm not bad and I'm still learning. You're fantastic though! Maybe you could teach me a thing or two." She beamed at him hopefully as he grinned at her with his megawatt smile.

"I'd love to teach you, anytime you like," Jason offered enthusiastically. "Actually, why don't I teach you Silent Lucidity right now, you know the song?"

Maria queried, "That's the one you've been playing? I'm a little bit familiar with it. You know it's got a really deep message to that song if you listen to the lyrics. Haunting." She looked contemplatively at him as she thought of the meaning.

Jason nodded and replied, "Oh yeah I'm well aware."

You could see that there was more to it than just awareness, a significant importance of some kind. Soon she would find out as the pair clicked instantly and became practically inseparable before long.

Girl and Boy Fall in Love

It had been several months since they first met and they spent every day together, every moment they could. They played music together, they shared their hopes and dreams.

He was lead guitarist in his rock band Blood Red Sky. She sang and played guitar writing folk pop songs similar to the style of Jewel. People even said Maria sounded a lot like her. They both hoped to make it big one day and they were doing everything they could to make that happen.

They also bonded over the fact that they had both lost a brother who was very dear to them. Jason had been very close to his brother, James, more like best friends as they were only a couple of years apart in age. James had taken his own life just about a year earlier and losing him had rocked Jason to his core.

Maria had admired and looked up to her big brother Bobby who died of a degenerative muscle disease he had been born with, Muscular Dystrophy. They were ten years apart in age but he had been the best big brother ever who adored his baby sister and the most loving and kind person she had ever known. She had lost him when she was just ten years old and she missed him dearly.

They had both had an extremely hard time dealing with these losses and in talking about this she found out the significance of the song he first taught her to play at the party where they first met. Silent Lucidity.

Apparently after his brother had passed he and his family experienced some interesting spiritual phenomenon. Lights burning out, an exploding light bulb, electrical components acting up, radios turning on and playing James' favorite songs or songs that had significant meaning. So Jason learned to lucid dream as a means of communicating with his deceased brother. He then taught Maria so that she could communicate with her brother Bobby. He told her that after James passed he and his mom promised that when either of them died they would also try to communicate with each other. Maria was fascinated by all of this and very much interested in these same things. Jason and Maria made their own pact to communicate with each other when the time should come that either of them leave this earth, though they certainly hoped that time wouldn't come until far in the future.

Boy Makes it Big

They had fallen madly in love by the time his rock band, Blood Red Sky, had been signed to a major record label later that year and then it was time for Jason to head out on the road to tour the world playing sold out venues.

Maria was excited for him and supportive and so happy that his dreams were coming true. Yes, she also dreamed of making it big and was getting better and better at playing guitar under her sweet Jason's tutelage but she hadn't gotten there quite yet. Even still, she was truly one hundred percent happy for his success.

When it was time to leave to go on tour, with mixed emotions Jason exclaimed, "I'm so excited for this but I hate that I can't bring you with me!"

Maria looked at her love and said supportively but with a hint of mourning as an undertone, "Babe it's okay, you'll only be gone for what, three months, right? No problem, I'll see you when you get back home." Then she joked with him and winked, "Well, that is if you aren't too big to remember little old me by then."

Underneath the supportiveness she couldn't help but be sad that she wasn't going to see him for months on end and worried about possible temptation on tour, not that she'd ever been given any reason to worry about him cheating but things can be crazy on the road like that, she had always heard stories about that. She didn't even want to mention that concern to Jason however because she knew he'd be hurt that it even crossed her mind. He was absolutely a hundred and ten percent madly in love with her just as she was with him. But she had always struggled with insecurities and lack of confidence issues. This was going to be a rough three months, but she just smiled through her concerns and pretended everything was perfectly fine. She knew she was being silly anyway, most likely.

"Oh very funny, you little brat," Jason joked with her, "Like I could ever forget you." Then he leaned in close and gave her a soft, sweet, passionate kiss full of longing and regret for having to leave her behind. If was almost as if a part of him felt like it could be their last kiss so when it naturally ended he pulled her back in for an even longer more passionate one. It went on as if forever and when their lips finally parted Maria was weak in the knees and you could tell just by looking at her.

"Wow," Maria sighed, "you've never kissed me like that!" She could tell something was going on in that brain of his.

Jason looked at her affectionately and said, "You are the love of my life, Maria and I will love you until the day I die and even beyond that. Please don't ever forget that. I love you!"

Maria now had tears welling up in the corners of her eyes as she bid her lover farewell, "I love you too, Jason, so much! I will be waiting right here for you."

And with that he grabbed his luggage, opened the door and walked out, not knowing it would be forever.

Girl Lets Her Insecurities Get to Her

Three months went by in a flash and when it was time for Jason to be heading back home from his tour Maria was so ready to see him. She had been riddled by her insecurities the entire time he was on the road and she was beyond ready for that to be done. She didn't know how she would be able to handle him being gone for another tour. That's when the phone call came in.

"Hey babe," Jason said excitedly when she answered the phone. "I've got some awesome news about the band, they are extending the tour so we will be gone for another three months and they want to do a bunch of press stuff and photo shoots in the meantime. Isn't that amazing?"

Maria recoiled at his words and had to regain her composure before responding so as not to allow herself to sound upset for his happiness, "Oh, yeah, that's uh, so great. Happy for you babe." But she didn't sound happy no matter how hard she tried to.

Jason could hear the sadness and worry and he was concerned. "Maria, is everything okay? I thought you'd be happy, it's what we've always wanted."

Maria managed to mask her negative undertones when she spoke this time, "Oh, of course I am, Jason, so thrilled for you, it's all of your dreams come true." Then she fibbed, "I'm just having a tough time at work right now is all, it'll be fine."

Jason still concerned asked, "Are you sure babe? You can tell me anything that's bothering you anytime you know? I sure do miss you."

The sadness returned to her voice now and unable to cover it up Maria repined, "I miss you too, so much." Tears had been welling up and she could no longer hold them back. Her voice thick with emotion she said woefully, "Sorry, it will be fine I promise."

But it would not be fine. The band became more and more successful and they were kept out on the road longer and longer and eventually Maria couldn't take the worry and insecurities and just all of it anymore and so she broke it off with her beloved Jason without even giving him a good reason why.

He was crushed. So was she. She didn't want to break

it off, she loved him so much but she was getting more and more upset due to her own insecurities but she refused to tell him that because she would never forgive herself if he gave up on his dreams to come home to be with her. She was not going to be that girl, and so she moved on. She forced herself to. Out of love for him and putting his happiness before her own.

Boy and Girl Go Off the Deep End

On tour Jason was devastated at being broken up with by Maria. He couldn't stop thinking about her. He tried calling her but she never answered or returned his calls, he filled up her voicemail, he tried contacting her friends and family but all they would tell him was that she didn't want to hear from him. It broke him.

Jason began binge drinking and drugging and eventually hooking up with groupies all to numb the pain. Maria would see articles in gossip magazines about his escapades and now all her insecurities were cemented and she believed he must have been cheating on her all along so she definitely wouldn't communicate with him now. She was heartbroken, he was heartbroken and it just spiraled out of control more and more from there.

Maria stopped even playing music, it reminded her too much of Jason. She too started drinking to numb the pain and then one night out at the bar singing karaoke she met Rob. He was handsome and charming and she was lonely and depressed.

He bought drink after drink for them both and then invited her to go home with him.

"You probably shouldn't be driving with all you've had to drink, why not take a cab with me and then I can bring you back to pick up your car tomorrow," Rob offered smiling devilishly.

Maria was so drunk she couldn't even think straight let alone drive her car and she knew it. "Um, yeah sure that's probably a good idea," she slurred.

And thus began a long and horribly abusive relationship. He was a cocaine addict and an angry drunk and he enjoyed knocking Maria around every chance he got. He also loved to rub in her face that Jason was messing around with all the groupies.

Rob taunted Maria, "Your precious Jason clearly never loved you. Tell me you don't think he was screwing those bimbos all along. Hell, he was probably cheating before he ever went out on the road too, right under your nose."

Maria cried and shouted at him, "You shut the hell up about Jason, you don't know him, you don't know anything you ass—"

And with that Rob abruptly cut her off by backhanding her hard across the face. He hit her so forcefully that she nearly fell over. That was just the first time of many more beatings to come.

Rob scowled and snarled at her, "You stupid bitch, don't you know that nobody has ever really loved you? And do you think you'd find anyone else if I ever left you? Hell no. Just look at you. You're pathetic, you disgust me!"

So many times he said these things to her until she began to believe it and so she stayed with him, becoming more and more broken all along.

Boy Gets Booted From the Band

Several more months went by with the downward spiral continuing and Jason eventually got kicked out of his band.

"I'm sorry, Jason, but until you get yourself cleaned up you are out of the band until further notice," said the angry voicemail from his manager. "If you manage to pull yourself together again then maybe you'll be lucky enough to be invited back in but until then you are out." And just like that he was out of the band.

"How the hell can I get fired from the band I started?" Jason thought out loud angrily. "Man, that is some bullshit!"

He had now lost completely everything he cared about. Now he was not just devastated, he was angry. Angry at the world. He trashed his hotel room, got arrested for being so drunk and causing chaos in public, got arrested again for punching a paparazzi. How had he gotten here? He couldn't figure it out.

He continued on this path for a good month or so and then finally he knew what he had to do. He had to get his life straight and go find Maria and win her back! That was the only way he would find his happiness again. She was his soul mate and he was beyond lost without her.

First he checked himself into rehab and went through a full program, he stopped all the drinking and drugs and of course there were no more groupies since he wasn't touring anymore. He paid all the fines he accrued from property damage and arrests and then he headed back home to Arlington, Washington to find Maria once he had all of his life back in order.

Boy Tries to Win Back Girl

"Maria, this is Jason. Please call me, I'm back home, I just got out of rehab and I need to see you, please," leaving another message on Maria's voicemail. Again he tried calling numerous times with no response.

Jason eventually managed to reach a friend who finally gave him some valuable information.

"Well, don't tell her I'm the one who told you or she will be pissed… but I know she's working at the Rome Restaurant and Bar on the closing shift and she's working tonight," Jaime informed him. "Seriously though, do not tell her I told you."

Jason replied appreciatively, "I truly can not thank you enough, you don't know how much this means to me."

Jaime then asked him curiously, "But tell me Jason, did you really cheat on her the whole time you were together? Because that really tore her up."

He was appalled by the question and responded in shock and disbelief, "What are you talking about? Why would she ever have ever gotten that idea?"

Jaime looked sadly at Jason realizing he was telling the truth, "I don't know what made her think that then, man, but she was sure of it and it broke her."

Jason still could not believe this was even a thought she could have had in her mind. "Wow," he lamented, "I have got to set the record straight."

Later that night Jason headed to the Rome Restaurant in downtown Arlington. He was on a mission. He had to win back his soulmate come hell or high water. He walked into the Restaurant with its dimly lit Italian decor and looked around but couldn't find her. One of the other waitresses could see he was looking for someone. She also looked as though she thought she recognized him but couldn't quite place him.

"Excuse me, sir," said the waitress, Sara. "Can I help you?"

Jason piped up hopefully, "Well yes, I'm looking for Maria, she works here."

Sara nodded and said, "Oh sorry, yeah she just got off work. Can I say who is looking for her?"

Just then she got a look of realization on her face

when she saw his band t-shirt and it clicked in her mind who he was. Before he could respond she snapped her fingers and said, "That's right, you're Jason Butler! The guitarist of Blood Red Sky."

She noticed Jason looking extremely disappointed that he'd just missed her and just then another look of realization came across her face as she remembered that Maria had mentioned having been his ex-girlfriend.

Jason quickly replied, "That's right, do you know when she will be working next?"

Now Sara was looking uneasy as she also remembered Maria mentioning how she was avoiding him but he looked so desperate she felt bad for him and she was a fan of his music too.

Looking slightly guilty Sara sighed and then responded, "Okay, I'm only telling you this because I enjoy your music and you seem like a decent guy." She paused, thinking whether she should actually tell him or not and after a brief moment she continued, "She works again on Friday night, however, you might find her just over in the bar right now if you're lucky." With that she smiled and winked at him.

Jason looking so appreciative and hopeful replied excitedly, "Oh man, thank you so much, I owe you an autographed copy of one of my cd's, any one you want, just say the word!"

In an instant he was rushing over to the bar in hopes to find his Maria.

Girl Turns Boy Down

In the bar room of the Rome Restaurant sat Maria, already with a healthy buzz even though she just got off work not even a half hour ago. She looked tired with dark circles under her eyes, she looked like she had been crying and it appeared that she had bruises on her face that she had poorly covered up with makeup but it didn't quite do the trick. Her eyes looked dull and lifeless and there was no trace of the beautiful smile Jason remembered, but she was still the most gorgeous woman in the world to him and his heart soared the moment he saw her. Then he remembered that his beloved had somehow gotten it into her mind that he had cheated on her and he became woeful again as he approached her, hoping against hope that she would hear him out and give him another chance.

With a wistful look he called out to her, "Maria, please talk to me, please give me a chance."

Maria looked up drunkenly from her cocktail and immediately scowled at Jason, shook her head, put her hand up in the air as if to say 'talk to the hand' and went back to drinking. She wanted nothing to do with him and that was obvious.

Jason cried desperately, "I don't understand what I've done wrong. What did I do so wrong? You never even told me why you were breaking up with me, and I love you more than life itself. You always use to tell me you felt the same so what happened to suddenly change that?"

He looked at her woefully, waiting for a response of any kind as she continued to ignore him but then she began to cry and all he wanted to do more than anything was to hold her and comfort her. Maria looked up at him with tears in her eyes and the look of hurt on her face made him want to cry for her.

With her body and voice shaking Maria cried angrily, "What happened? You have the nerve to ask me what happened? You never loved me, you lied and you cheated and I never want to see you again." She gave him one final look of disgust and then cast her eyes back downward towards her cocktail intending to ignore him again.

Jason was devastated all over again by her coldness

towards him. He never would have thought she would treat him that way after all they shared and the love they had for each other. He had no idea how she could have even thought he would ever cheat on her. That she could just throw it all away so carelessly, all the love they shared, all the wonderful times and memories, he just couldn't comprehend. But while he was saddened by all of this he wasn't going down without a fight. He had come all this way and he was going to find out what went wrong. He had to.

"Maria, what on earth are you even talking about? I would never dream of cheating on you. Dammit woman you are my entire world. More important than any fame or fortune or anything else," Jason pleaded with her. "There is not another woman in this world that could even compare to you. Where did you get the idea that I cheated and lied?"

He was beyond hurt that she could believe such a thing, but he was desperate to win her back. She wrinkled her face in disgust as she lifted her head up from her glass to glare at him once more.

She spat her words at him as she laid it all out on the table finally for once and for all, "I knew all along that it would turn sour when you left to go out on the road. I worried that you'd be tempted by groupies being gone out there for so long without me and then I saw it all in the gossip rags, you were hooking up with all these women on the road!"

Jason was getting angry now for being wrongfully accused now that the shock of the initial hurt was wearing off and he spat back at her, "Maria, that was only after you dumped me. It damn near killed me losing you. I never cheated on you but after you broke it off I was trying to do anything I could to kill the pain of losing you. I didn't even want to be touring anymore but at that point it was all I had left."

As she glared at him some more he looked at her pleadingly, longing for her to realize he was telling the truth, tears now running down his face and he wasn't even trying to wipe them away. Something finally clicked and her scowl began to fade into a look of remorse as she could see he was telling the truth. She began to remember all the love they shared and she knew his heart, his soul. She finally believed in their love once again and she began to sob uncontrollably.

Through her tears she apologized, "Oh god Jason, I'm so sorry what have I done to us? I'm so stupid and I should have told you my concerns instead of keeping them to myself and just letting it all fester in my mind."

Maria continued weeping as Jason approached her thankful he had finally gotten through. With open arms he embraced her and she leaned into him and cried her heart out.

Jason consoled his love, "It's okay I'm here now, we're together again. I love you always and forever, just like I told you, until I die and beyond."

Maria shook her head and sobbed, "No, this is all my fault, all the sorrow and all the pain, yours and mine. It's not okay and we can't be together because I moved on and I'm with another man now." She began to sob even harder upon revealing that.

Jason felt as though he had been stabbed in the chest and cried to Maria, "But what about us? What, are you saying you care for him more than all the love we shared?" He leaned in closer to her to help get it to sink in. "We're soul mates Maria, remember? You and me against the world for eternity and beyond?"

Maria looked at him woefully and simply said, "It doesn't matter, I'm with someone else." It killed her to say it. She didn't want to be with Rob anymore but she was afraid to leave and felt trapped because he threatened to kill her if she ever left him. She couldn't tell this to Jason or it could cause problems and she didn't want him getting hurt.

Jason then took a good look at her and seeing all the marks on her face he said, "Are those bruises? Is he hitting you? Who is he, I'll kill him!"

Maria shook her head sadly, "Just leave it alone Jason, I will love you always, but it's over between us."

Jason beside himself with sadness pleaded, "But why, Maria? It doesn't have to be."

Before Maria could respond, Rob walked into the bar high as a kite and sauced up to boot. He took one look at Jason standing close to Maria and he was fuming.

"Maria you get out to the car right now you stupid bitch, it's time to go home," Rob barked angrily.

Maria quickly got up and scurried out of the bar headed to Rob's car without uttering another word. Jason was instantly ready to fight him and even though Rob was much larger in stature, he was not going to stand for this.

"Who the hell do you think you are? You don't get to order her around like that," Jason growled fiercely.

"Oh yeah," Rob scoffed, "And what are you gonna do about it you stupid punk ass bitch?"

Jason didn't even bother to respond again, instead he punched Rob square in the nose, got him real good. Rob recoiled and grabbed Jason by the shirt and pushed him into a table knocking glasses all over the place and the few patrons in the bar backing off out of the way as it broke into a full on brawl. The bartender tried to break it up but couldn't manage to stop them or slow them down. Before long the police arrived and arrested them both as Maria sat in the car crying while they were each hauled away.

Girl Winds Up In Hospital

That very next day after the bar brawl, Maria bailed Rob out of jail for fear that he'd kill her when he got out if she didn't. Unfortunately he already wanted to kill her for Jason being there with her at the bar in the first place, so when he got home he was already all fired up.

"Welcome home Robby," she said nervously when he walked through the door.

Without even responding he sneered at her and then grabbed her by the hair as she screamed and begged him to stop. "Rob no, I didn't do anything I swear," Maria cried. "He just showed up out of the blue, I don't even know how he found me."

But he wouldn't hear it. He was seeing red and he meant to end her life right then and there. He dragged her over to the stairs and then bashed her head repeatedly into the steps while calling her every horrible name in the book as she screamed and cried until she was unconscious.

"Take that you whore, how dare you embarrass me!" He shouted at her as he continued to beat her even after she stopped fighting back.

In the hospital that night Jason visited but Maria was in a coma. The doctors said it didn't look good and he cried his eyes out unabashedly, holding her hand and begging for her to wake up.

"I just finally found you again," Jason cried, "Don't you leave me, please Maria!" Choking his words out through his tears he cried, "I can't live without you, please stay with me."

The tears eventually faded and he stayed by her side for days as the machines kept her alive, it seemed that she would never wake up but he never gave up hope. Then one day Rob showed up at the hospital, drunk, high and ready for a fight as usual. He found Jason in Maria's room and as soon as Jason took a look at Rob headed toward him and Maria the first thing he did was get up to keep Rob away from her, to protect her from any further harm.

Rob punched Jason knocking him down and before he could get back up Rob was at his throat strangling him.

"Die you asshole, this is all your fault," Rob shouted.

As this was going on the alarms on Maria's machines began to go off signaling the hospital staff.

Jason managed to break free momentarily. He heard the alarms and looked concerned towards his true love, he cried with fear that she was dying, "Maria, stay with me!"

That pissed off Rob even more and he was back at his throat, "You son of a bitch, she's mine!"

Jason tried to break away again but Rob was too strong and out for blood. Jason gurgled and sputtered as he struggled but it didn't take long before he stopped fighting back. Jason had been strangled to death just feet away from his beloved Maria, his soulmate.

A nurse heard all the commotion along with the alarm and was hurrying that way to see what was happening.

"Excuse me sir, what is going on," shouted the nurse. Rob looked guilty as sin and still furious. She then saw the dead body of Jason on the floor and screamed, "Help, code gray! We have a code gray in room two-seventeen!"

Rob heard the nurse shout and he was off and running down the hall, right into a police officer's tazer gun, he was down for the count.

The nurse had made it into the hospital room where Maria was finally waking up from her coma. She awoke to find her sweet beloved soul mate lying still on the floor and began flailing to get all the tubes out so she could go to him. The nurse ran to her.

"Miss, please stop fighting, I will safely disconnect your tubes when you are ready, please remain calm," warned the nurse. "Let me check on this young man, you please just try to calmly stay in your bed."

Maria stopped fighting as the nurse went to check for vital signs and she found that he was deceased. The nurse called for help and gave CPR and when help came they attempted to revive him for hours but he was gone and all Maria could do was cry for her love, dead on the floor, through the tubes in her throat.

Girl Communicates With Boy

Safe, alive, and out of the hospital, Maria was back at home while Rob was taken to jail where he sat awaiting trial for the murder of Jason and attempted murder of Maria. There was no way he wouldn't be convicted so Maria was truly safe from his abuse for once and for all.

With Jason gone, Maria was devastated but then funny things started happening. Lights began to turn on and off, sometimes they would glow extra bright. Electronics began misbehaving. The radio came on suddenly, only to play Silent Lucidity, she and Jason's special song. She smiled when she heard it. She knew it was her beloved making good on his pact to communicate with her and so now it was her job to lucid dream so she could communicate with him too.

"Hey babe, thank you for keeping your promise," Maria spoke to the empty room around her, "I will be contacting you in my dreams. I love you."

That night as she prepared to lay down to sleep she did all the things that Jason had taught her about how to lucid dream.

She closed her eyes and visualized the party at Pilchuck River, that fateful day where they first met. And there she was together with her Jason, her one true love, her soul mate. As if they'd never been apart. He was sitting there playing his guitar, of course he was playing that same song, smiling that adorable smirky smile, his signature smile that she loved so much.

The only difference from the party was that it was just the two of them now, alone together to say all the things they didn't get to say before he died.

"I'm so sorry babe, I messed everything up so bad," Maria apologized. "I should have just told you I was feeling insecure but I didn't want to ruin your happiness with all of your dreams coming true by making you worry about that. I couldn't do that to you."

Jason just smiled understandingly at Maria who continued on to say, "Of course, now I see it would have been better if I did tell you. I just wish I could go back and fix it."

He smirked again and said, "You can still fix it, babe. Want me to tell you how?"

Maria's eyes widened and she exclaimed, "Of course I want you to tell me how!"

Jason gave that smirky smile again and explained it all to her. He talked about how the first thing she needed to do was to get back to playing music, and that she should find some band mates. Put an ad in the Stranger classifieds looking for people to form a band with. He said he knew she would wind up where she is supposed to once she finds the right people to make music with.

He also told her how he would be there with her every step of the way and she would know when she found the right musicians.

"But what about fixing things for you and me, that's all that matters to me," Maria said sadly. She thought it was nice and all that he was encouraging her to follow her dreams but right now these dreams with Jason were the only ones she cared about.

"I can't tell you the specifics right now, babe but don't worry about that, I promise it will all be okay, trust me," he explained, squeezing her hand for comfort. "I am going to be moving into a new body, my same soul just different packaging. It will still be me in there though. Pay attention and you will know when we meet again."

Maria looked sadly at her love and then threw her arms around him crying into his shoulder until he lifted her chin up to kiss her. That same soft, sweet, passionate kiss she remembered and it all felt so real.

She pleaded with him, "Why can't we just stay here together forever?"

He smiled with a hint of sadness and replied, "We just can't. If we could I absolutely would. But trust me about the ad in the Stranger, you won't be disappointed."

He pulled her close and kissed her once more and then the dream was over. When Maria woke in the morning she felt a sense of peace and hope that she hadn't felt for so long.

Girl Meets Bandmate

Maria heeded Jason's words from their lucid dream meeting and posted an ad in the classifieds looking for band members and it didn't take long before the calls started coming in so she set up a day and times to meet with potential band mates. The very first audition meeting was with a guitarist. His name was Billy. He was tall and had short dark hair, bright blue eyes and a strangely familiar smirky smile.

"Hi Billy, pleased to meet you, thanks for responding to the ad," Maria stated pleasantly.

It wasn't just the smile that was familiar there was something else but she couldn't quite put her finger on it.

"Would you like to play a song for me," she asked Billy, "show me what you've got?"

Billy gave that same familiar smirky smile and said, "Absolutely, tell me what you think of this."

He began to play, it was a song she knew all too well. Silent Lucidity, of course.

for Billy, my kindred spirit

RAISING THE FOUR ELEMENTS
David Fuller

Once Upon a Time

There once was a charming Bard who married a brilliant Wizard. They were a young couple, new to the adventuring life without many plans, but full of life. Initially, things were perfect, and though they struggled at times, they struggled together. But their time together was not to last. A dark affliction infected the Bard's mind, making him think sad, worrisome thoughts. Seeking happiness and a way to fight his mind's darkness, the Bard asked the Wizard to cast a powerful spell that gifted him two elemental children, Earth and Water; spirits that would both occupy his time and challenge him to learn to be stronger so he could fight off the infection. The children added joy, but also new challenges that the immature Bard did not predict.

The Great Divide

Sometime after Earth and Water were summoned, the Bard left on a grand adventure to fight for the kingdom. He went out of love and a desire to find the gold and treasures it cost to raise growing elements. The time away hurt the Bard's heart significantly. He missed Earth's first days at school with other children. He missed when Water first learned how to make waves and was not there when she learned most of her words. The Bard was sad and lonely since he loved Earth and Water, but could not be there. Eventually, a time came in the adventure when the Wizard loaded up their things and brought the young elementals to where the Bard was staying. The Bard and Wizard decided it was better for the family to be together on an adventure. The Bard and the Wizard were still very young at this time and did not know what troubles were ahead.

It did not take very long for the stress of the adventurer's life to start to create a divide between the Bard and the Wizard. The Bard tried to focus on slaying monsters and completing quests so he could show his love through service and, in his pride, thought that was enough. The Bard and the Wizard started to argue about everything, from how to best take care of the elements to how much time the Bard was spending time with friends. It was a dark time for the Bard, and he failed to give Earth and Water the love they deserved. Eventually, the Wizard decided that the elements would be better raised elsewhere and took them from the Bard. The Bard was sad and lonely for some time and missed much of the young element's lives.

In time the Bard met a brave Warrior, and they fell in love. With the support of the Warrior, the Bard finished his battles for the kingdom and returned to the land where the Wizard was keeping the elements. The Bard and Warrior worked to settle in as retired adventures, and life was hard for a while, but worth it because the Bard was finally back in Earth and Water's lives. The Bard worked with the Wizard and agreed on equally dividing the time the elements spent with each of them. This arrangement did not initially change the Bard's love for the young elements, but the great divide taught the Bard to make family a higher priority in their life.

The great divide did bring another unexpected challenge. Eventually, the Wizard met and fell in love with a Warlock, and he started to help raise Earth and Water. The Bard thought this would not impact him much, but as time passed, the Bard began to notice little changes. Earth and Water would talk about how much fun they had with the Warlock and the Bard became intensely jealous. The jealousy caused his affliction to worsen, until a moment of clarity helped him to learn that the most valuable treasure was the elementals' happiness, no matter where they found it. He could see that the Warlock had come to love the elementals just as the Warrior had and that his children were truly blessed to be loved by so many. The Bard learned not to make things about himself so that he could be happy for Earth and Water.

Over the years, the elementals developed unique personalities and a diverse range of interests. The Bard learned that he needed to love them all in different ways, and in turn, learn new ways to love himself and fight his affliction.

Earth: The Element that is Strong and Stubborn

When Wizard cast the first spell, the Bard searched the halls and chambers of his estate. The first elemental he found was his son, Earth, getting dirt all over the pages of books in the castle library. Earth was a focused element, absorbing knowledge wherever it presented itself. The Bard was thrilled to have a son that was so brilliant. He encouraged Earth's passions and was excited to see what the future had in store for the messy learner. During those early years, the Bard could not spend as much time with his son as his heart wanted. Monsters needed to be slain, and dungeons needed to be liberated of their treasures. The Bard wished to know his son but allowed himself to be distracted by the business of an adventurer's life, confident that the Wizard was giving Earth enough attention. This led to many scary moments in young Earth's life, as Earth would get into things a small elemental shouldn't play with, like kitchen knives. Earth managed to make it through his earliest years in one piece, and the Bard learned that he had to always be vigilant if he was going to keep his little element safe.

Before he knew it, the Earth elemental had grown to the point that it needed to get outside the castle walls if it was going to keep learning, so the Bard and Wizard looked into the best magical schools he could. The first one he sent Earth too was not very accepting of elementals, specifically ones that left dirt everywhere they went. The supposedly healthy children were upset at the mess, and the teachers objected to having to take extra time with Earth. By this time, the great divide had happened, so the Bard was only able to offer support from afar and did not appreciate how hard things were for Earth and the Wizard. Later, when the Bard looked back, he felt terrible that he was not nearer at the time.

Worried that Earth would run into the same problems at his next magical school, the Bard and Wizard researched how to make it so Earth would not leave dirt on things he touched. Every book about elementals said the same: Earth would always make a little bit of a mess, he was just how he was, and they would have to learn how to accept it. Thinking a little dirt here and there was easy enough to adjust to, they pushed on and found Earth another magical school. This one was filled with a variety of magical creatures and had specialized professors devoted to cleaning up the dirt Earth couldn't help leave on his seats, books, and other students. The Bard was happy and felt that everything was going to work out for Earth, but he had more to learn about being a father to an Earth elemental. Earth learned differently than the other students in his school, focusing on one task at a time and getting frustrated when he had to divide his attention or work out multiple steps at once. These frustrations would manifest as Earthquakes that sometimes scared the other magical creatures and human students. The Bard and Wizard tried to work with Earth to better understand what was creating these problems, but they did not know how to relate; the Bard was saddened that his love for Earth was not enough to get the child what he needed.

Feeling lost, the Bard had to accept that all of his songs, magic, and lore would not always defeat every challenge or slay every monster. The Bard worked with the Wizard to get help for Earth. The magic school provided as much support as they could, and the Bard and Wizard found experts in Earth elemental care. These specialists worked with Earth to identify why he sometimes caused quakes and often left dirt on things. The conclusion was that Earth would always interact with others differently, and it was no one's fault.

Life continued to be challenging for Earth and his parents, but time did pass, and the elemental grew tall and strong, even becoming more massive than the Bard. As Earth grew, he became interested in a broader range of subjects, from wondrous monsters to the thrills of adventures. The Bard was overjoyed that Earth not only had things he was excited about, but he seemed to enjoy interest similar to his own. A new challenge arose in loving Earth: while most people would get excited about things, Earth would attack the subject matter, consuming it in its entirety. Once he knew everything there was to know about a subject, Earth made sure everyone else knew about it. Bard loved how passionate Earth would get and listened to the same factoids and "Hey, did you know…" dozens of times, but eventually subjects would need to change. Earth always seemed a little disappointed that the Bard asked him to stop talking, and the father was afraid he was not listening enough or giving his oldest son enough attention. The Bard learned that loving someone that sees the world the way Earth does require patience and understanding, but also a level of self-awareness that the Bard did not initially possess. The Bard had to learn that he cannot punish himself for not having unlimited time to spend with his son.

Eventually, Earth became almost old enough to leave the castle and go off on his own adventures. The Bard was both excited and scared for his oldest son. Years of working with Earth elemental experts and going to magic schools helped Earth learn how to better take care of himself, but he still left dirt on things and even caused the occasional quake. One day Earth admitted he was scared to go off on his own; tears turned his face to little mudslides. The Bard sat with his son and assured him that Earth is strong and steady. The Bard hoped that everything would be okay, but part of loving a child is having fear for their future while being excited about their potential.

Water: The Element that is Deep and Powerful

The second elemental that the Bard and Wizard summoned was the crystal clear Water. Water did not enter the world easily, and she spent her first moments in the world splashing around in the Bard's arms while healers ran to the Wizard's side. In her efforts to bring Water into the world, the Wizard had damaged something inside her and was losing life quickly. Chaos and fear swarmed around the Bard, but all of that faded while he looked down at the peacefully resting elemental. The heartache in the background resolved itself while the Bard whispered reassurances to his newly summoned daughter. The healers eventually broke his peaceful trance to assure him that the Wizard was going to be okay and just needed rest.

The Bard took Water and the Wizard back to the castle to meet Earth. Earth was still very young and welcomed another elemental to play with; this attitude would change with time. Like many siblings, Earth and Water would eventually grow to be annoyed by each other: where Earth stayed rigid, Water would flow and adapt. The Bard missed the earliest years of Water's life either through focusing on the life of adventure or too much time with his friends. Later, the Bard's heart would become heavy when looking back, and he wished he could have approached things differently, but time travel is beyond even the greatest Wizard's powers. Thanks to the Wizard, the Bard was provided many updates on Earth and Water's development, so he at least had that to hold.

After the Great Divide, the Bard was far away from Water but still worked hard to travel to the castle and see her. Each time she was a little bigger than before, more curious and more talented. Water was a fearless elemental that would flow up to strangers and ask them to read her books or give friendly smiles to people she passed while swimming around town. Water was a social creature, just like the Bard, and he couldn't help but feel proud of her. Everyone commented on how her personality was just like his, and it was easier to relate to her than Earth. It was not always a good thing as Water also had some of the Bard's more manipulative personality traits. When she went off to magic school, she started bossing people around and getting into fights. The problem came home as Water watched the adults struggle with Earth; she began to correct him as if she was the parent. The Bard had to frequently remind Water that she was not the adult, which seemed to confuse and hurt her.

As Water became older, she kept trying to take on more responsibilities than anyone expected of her. It seemed to the Bard that Water was being bossy or controlling, and he discouraged much of the behavior or brushed it aside. The Bard had no idea that the same darkness inside of him polluted the waves in Water's mind. One night when the Bard and Warrior were entertaining friends after the elementals had begun to rest, Water came into the room, leaving wet tears in her wake. Water had poisoned herself and needed help. Terrified, the Bard and Warrior rushed Water to healers. The Wizard came, and everyone tried to figure out how things got to this point. The healers needed to keep Water for a night, so the Bard stayed with his daughter and kept her company. That night he realized he would remain by his children's side forever if needed to keep them safe.

Over the next few months, Water would work with the healers and the adults in her life to find ways to help fight the darkness. It would always be a struggle, but Water's family would not let her give up. The adults in her life would spend extra time with her so she wouldn't be alone or provide opportunities for her to socialize with other students from the magical school. Despite these efforts, Water would still have times when the darkness would take control of her mood. Water would eventually need more help from healers, but her family was always there, and she always came back home to the castle.

As Water kept growing, she developed impressive artistic talents. The Bard and Warrior hung her art on the castle walls and provided her supplies to let her practice her craft and hone her skills. As the Bard was a bit of a storyteller, he had the idea of working with Water. He would provide the stories, and she illustrated them. Initially, this worked very well, but the Bard realized that this created a bit of conflict between Water and himself. While she was passionate about her art, she lacked the maturity and focus that comes with age. Sometimes the two had frustrated exchanges when

Water would fail to provide promised artwork, and the Bard worried about placing too much pressure on her young shoulders. Water and the Bard eventually finished the books they were working on, but the Bard was never sure if the stress was worth it.

Water continued to develop and grow, and the time came that she was getting closer to leaving for her own adventures. Unlike Earth, Water seemed better prepared for future adventures far away from home, but the Bard was still concerned about how she would handle the darkness when she was on her own. Like with Earth, the Bard had to learn to prepare the one he loved as best as he could. She would not be in the castle forever, and he had to accept it.

Air: The Element that is Everywhere

Eventually, the Bard and the Warrior decided their home was too empty during the times Earth and Water were not there. They chose to perform the same spell that created the two other elements, but this time an Air and a Fire elemental entered their lives. The first time the Bard looked at the little ball of Air, he was surprised to see how curious and aware the tiny element appeared. Within moments of entering the world, he was already looking around, exploring everything with his cloud-like eyes. Air was a happy element, and as the Bard watched, Air grew and grew, and as he grew, his energy increased; kinetic energy just waiting to be released. Sometimes he would be a dancing breeze, other times a sudden gust, and still sometimes a terrible tornado of emotion.

The Bard loved to watch Air fly through the house. Walls would shake as Air flew past paintings and decorations. From time to time, things would break in the gusts that followed. The Bard had to learn to care less about the things that he owned as Air's energy meant everything in the house was in danger at all times. Air would often pick up small objects in his wake and fling them across the room with a startling crash. One such time an expensive viewing glass that the Bard used to watch stories was shattered by such an object. The elemental knew he had done something terrible, and rain poured from his cloudy eyes as he raced to the Bard crying about the accident. The Warrior took Air aside while the Bard went to examine the viewing glass. The mirror surface had a spider web pattern that made watching stories impossible. The Bard wanted to scream, but to love the Air is to accept that sometimes accidents happen, sometimes things break, and the Air did not mean it. Even though the Bard did not let Air know that he was angry about the glass, the little elemental could still tell he had done something to upset his father.

After the incident with the viewing glass, Air was a little more cautious, more worried about his actions. The Bard noticed Air became nervous about things small elemental shouldn't worry over. The Bard and the Warrior worked together to help Air regain his confidence, but only time would repair the damage. The Bard felt responsible; his anger over a child damaging a material thing seemed to have taught the elemental a fear he had not previously known. Whether or not this was the Bard's fault, his dark affliction reared its ugly head and whispered nasty words to him. The Bard started to over-think his impact on all the elementals, and the Darkness fed on his growing anxiety.

With time Air recovered and returned to his curious, energetic self. Life was pretty good for the happy elemental, but then Fire was summoned. At first, Air was excited about the new family member, but it did not take long for Air to notice that people were giving more attention to the tiny new embers. Air discovered jealousy for the first time, and he started to act out. Air would purposefully play with Fire's toys or would try to take other people's chairs at dinner. The Bard was an only child, so he was not immediately aware of why Air was acting this way, but the Warrior had multiple siblings, so she recognized the behavior. Warrior was able to explain what was happening to the Bard. To help reduce these conflicts, the Bard had to learn how to be mindful of the love and affection he was giving to his two youngest. He worked to make it clear that he loved them both equally and while it did not make Air's relationship with Fire perfect, it helped reduce the amount of conflict between the siblings. Air still wanted a large amount of the Bard's attention, so there would always be times when Air demanded the Bard's time and though it broke his heart, the Bard would have to inform Air that he did not have time to play. Part of becoming a better parent involved learning not to hate himself for failing to have infinite time.

As Air continued to grow and started to attend the magical schools, a few things became apparent. First off, Air's movements were all over the place. The elemental would blow through the castle, running into things and knocking stuff over. Second, Air was brilliant, even compared to the other elementals. To gain better control of his movements, the Bard and Warrior found a school focused on dancing. Air took to the new actively immediately and started to practice his new skills all around the castle. The training helped Air not destroy things or himself.

To help encourage the growth of Air's intelligence, the Bard and the Warrior provided puzzles and games that challenged the elemental's mind. Everything from games involving telling stories to problems that demanded Air master light mazes. The Bard and the Warrior also answered all of Air's questions about the world around him, no matter how deep or complicated. The various experiences provided to Air gave birth to a desire to do everything possible and perform every task when he became a full-grown elemental. While others responded that he should choose a more realistic goal, the Bard learned that encouraging Air's dreams was the best way to love him. Air danced like a summer breeze, light and fast and beautiful, flitting from room to room almost as fast as he moved from idea to idea.

Fire: The Element that Lights and Burns

The story of Fire is the shortest the Bard has, but that is only because Fire is still a small elemental. The Bard was busy with Earth, Water, and Air as well as a few quests he still managed to fit into his life. Even with all of that, the Bard and the Warrior wanted to summon one more element to care for and love. They took the time to prepare, and when everything was right, they cast the spell. Fire came into the world in a much greater rush than those before her. The ritual was exhausting on the Warrior and made her very sick, but ultimately proud to meet the new elemental girl. Fire was a beautiful elemental; whose flames were the red-orange of the Warrior's hair. She knew how to hold other's attention with a smile or a sly look. She had the Warrior's beauty and the Bard's charisma, a deadly combination indeed. Everyone who met her loved Fire, and she quickly became the center of attention.

By the time the Bard had helped summon Fire, he was getting a little older, and keeping up with the small flame was exhausting. The Bard's back would freeze up in pain, and his knees would pop as he climbed the castle stairs, but little Fire would still need holding. The Bard found that he had less energy to devote to Fire than he wanted. The elemental taught the Bard that he had physical limits, and that he was done summoning new elementals into his life. The realization was a bit painful as the Bard found more meaning in loving others than he ever did loving himself. Ultimately the Bard had to realize that one cannot make others responsible for his happiness, and this helped him love everyone in his life unconditionally.

The Bard discovered that watching Fire was fascinating and filled him with joy. Fire was curious about the world around her, and so much was new to her. She viewed things with fresh optimism, and it helped the Bard remember to love the world around him. The optimism inherent in such a young elemental corrected many of the lies the darkness had told the Bard. While life could be difficult sometimes, the Bard knew that there were always things to be grateful for and love. Fire could burn away dark thoughts with her ever-present warmth.

Finally, while Fire did not have many adventures with the Bard, she did provide an opportunity for the other elementals to develop and learn. By the time Fire was summoned, Earth and Water were old enough that they could be trusted with watching their smaller sibling while the Bard and Warrior were busy with adventures or just keeping the castle cleaned. Earth was nervous about how to best take care of Fire and took a while to get comfortable around the warm elemental. Eventually, he gained the confidence he needed and started playing with Fire without being afraid he would break her. Somewhat ironically, considering their elements, Water took to Fire rather quickly. Except for the times the darkness crept into her mind, Water would take care of Fire if the Bard and Warrior needed her to with enthusiasm.

Fire could be a handful, but everyone loved the little elemental and ultimately were happy to help her through the adventure called life. Her approach to life was fearless and daring, and though she could rage as hot and fierce as an inferno, she most loved to cuddle up and share her warmth with everyone around her.

How to Love Others While in Darkness

The Bard always struggled with darkness but spent much of his life ignoring it. The unhealthy decision led to the Bard being rude and sometimes cruel to people around him when he felt an unexplained pain. The darkness eventually ended his adventuring career, which ultimately allowed him to return home to his children. The affliction made it difficult for the Bard to keep work around the village, making his self-worth drop with each failed attempt to care for the elementals. On the days when the darkness had the most significant hold on his mind, the Bard had difficulty getting out of bed. He felt terrible about not being there for the elementals and putting all of the responsibility of managing the castle on the Warrior's shoulders.

The darkness was an insidious enemy that crept into the Bard's mind with little warning. His days would begin like any other, but then things would start to change. The Bard's energy fell away, and the scale of happy to sad shifted so his default mood became a dour gray. The Bard tried many different types of potions and met with expert healers to discuss how the affliction altered his feelings. These things helped, but nothing could completely keep the darkness from entering his thoughts and filling him with self-doubt. It also made it difficult for the Bard to communicate with both the elementals and the Warrior. Countless times the Warrior attempted to find out what was wrong with the Bard's mood, but the darkness cluttered his words, so he was not able to describe what was troubling him.

The darkness also impacted the Bard's attempts at growing his career. Self-doubt and anxiety would cause the Bard to over examine every little thing his peers or superiors said to him. Every difficulty would transform into a mountain inside of his mind. It was a mountain that he could not climb, no matter how hard he tried.

As the elementals grew older, the Bard noticed how his affliction impacted them. Earth struggled to understand people around him, and so he was often confused when the darkness infected the Bard's mind. Water and Air were bright; both noticed and worried when the Bard was struggling, and it hurt the Bard in his heart. Children should not need to worry about their parent's wellbeing. Fire was still too young to understand what was wrong with the Bard, but she knew when those around her were "sick" and tried to spread her light and warmth even when the Darkness was too deep for the littlest elemental. The Bard regretted the time darkness stole from his family. He learned that being honest with them about his fight with the darkness in his mind was the only way to let them see that while he was sick, it was not their fault, and he still loved them.

Learning to Love Equally, but Different

The Bard now has four elementals that are his children, all different, but all deserving love and affection. The challenges the Bard faced in his life, both related to and separate from the elementals have shaped him and helped him love others and himself better. A father never has a favorite child, just favorite aspects, memories, feelings tied to each. The Bard loves Earth for his innocence, his imagination, and his unmatched enthusiasm when it comes to the subjects he cares about. As the child becomes an adult, the Bard wonders how he can still help direct Earth to hopefully make his first years away from home as painless as possible. Water is the child that is the most like the Bard. On most days, her personality not only commands the room but leads others to be entertained and joyous.

On the other days, the same darkness that haunts the Bard's mind infects Water, and she is moody and self-critical. Like the Bard, she is artistic; while he weaves stories, she brings pictures to life. Loving Water has helped the Bard learn to love himself more. Air is the first the Bard got to see completely through his earliest years. The joy that elemental brings to the Bard's life is immeasurable and so precious that the Bard's heart sinks anytime Air is sad or sick. In a perfect world, the Bard would give Air everything he wanted and keep him safe and happy all the time, but Air has helped the Bard learn that love means wanting to give a child everything, but knowing what they need. And finally, the Bard loves Fire because she loves the world around her.

Things are still new and wondrous and it helps remind the Bard that the world is magic. Love is the magic that makes all the challenges and trials of raising the four elements worth it.

Lay Down
Marshall Miller

All right people, hurry it up. We don't have all day."

The six teenagers grumbled and complained as their large work supervisor used his booming voice to remind them they were expected to work. Thomas Washington was a black man with the build of an NFL lineman. He wore a windbreaker stretched to its limits with 'Juvenile Probation' printed in large yellow letters on the back.

The six juveniles were trying to expend the least energy possible as they went about cleaning the community cemetery. However, this was not the first day of Tom as their supervisor. Nor would it be their last.

Susie Peele made a production of tying back her long cheerleader blonde hair as the other girl in the group, a young black girl named Megan Whitehouse, frowned as she tried to remove something from her fingernails. The jock Tim Knight kept trying to conceal his muscular frame behind whatever tree or clump of brush he could. Except for when he could find an excuse to pose in front of the two attractive young women.

Nick D'Amico glared at everyone and everybody. The Wheeler brothers, Mike and Mack, two stereotypical rednecks who wore sloppy jeans and t-shirts as if to say, hey, we were born in the South and proud of it. Yet, both had been born in the Northwest.

Thomas sighed in frustration. He had accepted taking on this group of malcontents after the High School Vice Principal, Julia Stindel, had asked him as a personal favor.

"Tom, this is it for these teens," Julia had said with a worried frown. *"That last series of stunts they pulled have the Principal and the local County Prosecutor seeing red."*

"So, they agreed to community service to time in Juvie?"

"Yes, thank God." Julie chewed on her bottom lip, a sign just how worried she was about the six kids. Tom knew her from his days in the military. Marines, to be exact. They had met in the Sandbox and kept in touch ever since. He knew that Julie's slender frame hid a wiry strength that surprised most. Tom had seen the dark-haired woman in action. For her to be worried, meant something to Tom.

"Okay. If Juvenile Probation signs off on it, I'm your huckleberry."

Which happened. And now for the last two weeks, Tom had been trying to impress on the six so-called young adults some concepts of personal responsibility and work ethic past just 'what's in it for me?'

Thus, when the local Evergreen Cemetery had asked for help in cleaning up the graves and grounds, he had jumped at it. Time to make these six brats confront the possibility of their own mortality.

Tom herded the two young women to pick up another couple of garbage bags from the oversized van. He gave Tim a scythe to use on some very overgrown bushes, as the other three young males wore gloves and picked up a myriad of old cigarette butts, discarded vape pens, and condoms.

"Who would want to screw in a cemetery?" grumbled Nick as he picked up several used condoms.

"Ask Megan 'n Susie," said Mike. "Rumor is, they were caught runnin' nekkid through the woods nearby."

Tom overheard the comment and intercepted any attempt to start a conflict. "Belay that question, Nick. If they want to say why they are on this work detail, they'll tell you."

"Ah, Mister Washington. You're spoiling our fun," said Mack.

"Since when is this supposed to be fun? You want fun? I can send you to Juvie and—"

"Forget I said anything. I was just jokin'."

Tom shook his head. The fake down-home accents the Wheeler Brothers affected were wearing thin. Just then, the two young ladies sauntered up.

"Ah, back at last, I see," said Tom. "Do you ever move fast?"

Meghan and Suzie looked at each other and shrugged.

"They do when they run nekkid!" The falsetto voice came from one of the Wheeler brothers. Tom's back was to them, so he could not tell which one, as both were clowns who acted the fool whenever the chance presented itself. Tom turned and glared at them as Nick snickered. Susie gave the two brothers the one-fingered salute, which made Nick, Mike, and Mack all laugh.

"Alright, comedy hour is over. Susie, Megan, start with those graves over there. Pick up any dead flowers, trash, you know the drill."

Tom glanced over to where Tim was slashing brush and weeds. "You need another trash bag, Tim?"

"Nah. I have a spare." As he answered, the muscular jock started to remove his polo shirt.

"Keep it on, Knight. The ladies can't remove theirs,

and you are all in this together. Same rules for all, which is something you should learn."

"It would break the monotony if we played Shirts and Skins," interjected Nick. The Wheelers began to snicker, and Tim grinned as he flexed his muscles.

"You wouldn't know what to do with a nice set of tits," sneered Megan. "We know you all like flat-chested little boys."

"All right! That is enough." Tom reduced the possible bellow to a loud voice.

"Try to act like young ladies and gentlemen. Keep it up, and I'll ask Probation to keep you with me for another week to teach you all some decent manners. Got it?"

There was a series of grumbled 'yes' and 'yeahs.' Tom tried not to sigh with exasperation and somehow succeeded. These kids had been with him for a week, and he felt like they were just doing time to keep out of a stay in Juvenile Hall. All were seventeen, which meant they had the desires and equipment legal adults had but were not supposed to use it. Tom did know why everyone was here. Megan and Susie had been caught nude and intoxicated in a car Susie had 'borrowed' from her aunt. They would not say why they were sans clothes when the cops found them, although Tom believed they may have been experimenting with their sexuality. When the former Marine was growing up, you expected to find Susie the Cheerleader making out with Tim the Jock behind the bleachers. Now, it seems everyone was trying to discover what orientation they were through acts of exploration. Not for the first time did Tom think he had grown up in an easier, more simple time compared to these kids.

Tom Washington kept them working for another hour before he broke them for lunch. He had brought the makings for sandwiches as well as some soft drinks, with a small budget from Probation footing the bill. Tom set up a folding table and set out all the fixings for lunch.

"Here, young ladies and gentlemen. You may fix your

own sandwiches, so no one claims I am poisoning them. Wash your hands with water from the Gott, then use whatever lunch meat you want. Chips and sodas are over there."

The six soon proved the old adage that teenagers are always hungry. As he watched them eat and actually joke a bit with each other, Tom had hope that he was actually accomplishing a bit of positive socialization so that they would not be such angry young people. Tom knew from his own experience that being angry growing up was easy. Being happy was harder.

"Judging by the amount you are eating, I'll have to do some more shopping."

"Hey, boss, why not just take us to a fast food place?" asked Nick. "It's quick, and we can order what we want."

"Because, this is cheaper, and it is actually quicker. So, who can do the math to show I'm right?"

"Nick didn't figure in the time to and from," answered Mike. "Eating sandwiches we make here, we stay here at the job. Not to mention less gas usage."

"Look at the brain on the redneck brother," quipped Tim. "Are you the smart one, or are you adopted?"

"Hey, Mister Knight, let's not get nasty about people's heritage and personality," said Tom. "Or are you going to start making using certain words that begin with 'f' and 'n' which will result in you spending more time with me?"

The jocks face reddened. He did not like to be called out in front of others.

"Just don't call me a Spic or a Wop, buddy," said Nick. "My *family* might take offense."

People began to snicker as Tom looked at Nick.

"Did anyone ever tell you that the 'Godfather' series is out of date?" the former Marine asked. "Most so-called enforcers these days are from South of the Border, Russia, or are Islamic fundamentalists. Not to mention that you are no way related to any of the traditional criminal families of yore."

"Hey, a guy can dream, can't he?" Nick replied with a

half-smile.

"Okay, finish up, then back to work, There are some public toilets the Army Corps of Engineers built some years back if you need to relieve ourselves. They are over close to the small Veterans Section."

"I'm going," said Suzie, and Megan followed her.

"Alright. Don't dally, as my Grandma used to say."

"Yeah, no playing hide the finger," said Mike as Mack laughed.

"Manners, gentlemen, manners. Or you'll be joining Tim for some extra socialization education."

Tom supervised the four males in cleaning up the lunch stuff as they griped about the women using a potty break to get out of work when they heard a scream, then an angrily yelled curse from the toilets. Tom was off like a shot as he yelled at the others to stay put. The restrooms were some one hundred yards away, which Tom crossed in record time. He rounded the corner of the building and almost ran over Suzie.

"What happened?" Tom demanded.

"Just some old homeless piece of shit hanging around the lady's room. We threatened to kick his ass, and he took off."

"Where?"

"Over there," Megan said as she pointed. Tom looked where the teenager pointed and saw the falling down metal arch that marked the entranceway to the small Veterans grave area. Just then, Tim slid to a stop next to Tom.

"I thought you might need backup," Tim said when he saw Tom's glare.

"Listen. Stay Here. Got it?"

Tom left the three youths standing and grousing as he trotted over to the Veterans Graves. This area was one of the most neglected areas of the Evergreen Cemetery, with vines and tall brush growing in abandoned. Tom made his way through the overgrown archway and soon saw the supposed homeless person. The man had a tangled beard and equally tangled long hair. As Tom neared, he saw the man was dressed in some ancient and faded BDUs. Tom made a slow approach to the man who was now kneeling by one specific grave.

"Excuse me, sir, but you upset the two young ladies…" Tom stopped in the mid statement as he noticed the name on the gravestone.

Michael S. Muller. USMC.

"Can't be," Tom mumbled as he checked the dates on the gravestone. They fit like a glove to what he was thinking.

"Just visiting an old friend," the disheveled man said as he placed some wildflowers on the grave, then turned to look at Tom.

Beneath the dirt, grime, and matted hair was an eerily familiar face. Tom's mind could not put a name with the visage. Then the homeless man helped.

"Sergeant Washington, is that you?"

All six of the youthful offenders wound up standing by the public toilets, grumbling about why their supervising adult was off talking to some homeless derelict. Suddenly, Tom was striding towards his charges.

"What happened?" asked Megan.

"Nothing. You startled the man as much as he did you. We'll get to the Veterans tomorrow." The former Marine glanced towards the beat-up archway. "The man is just paying his respects to a former comrade."

Tim Knight snorted.

"Yeah, right. Why is it everyone claims to be a homeless Vet when they want something? Hell, my Dad is a retired Colonel, and it's no big deal. All he does is drink and used to beat my Mom and me until I got older—and bigger."

"Your experience does not fit all Veterans. But now I know where your anger and chip on the shoulder come from."

Tim's face reddened.

"Oh yeah? Well, what, did you and mister stinky over there have a nice warm reunion…"

Tom's face was suddenly and inch from the jock's.

"Your mouth is about to write a check your ass can't cash. The worst that will happen to me if I clean your clock is I'll get fired. You'll get stuck with someone else on the way to the cold bar hotel."

"Hey, guys, can we stop this?" It was Suzie speaking. "I want to get off this detail someday. And, Tim, my mom's a Vet, so eff you."

Tom took a deep breath and stepped back. Then he pointed back to the department van.

"Go back there and finish clearing up the gravesites near the van. Move."

The six highschoolers went where Tom had pointed and said nothing more. They could tell Tom Washington was in no mood for any backtalk.

Tom's wife, Jenine, shook him awake. He jerked up in a cold sweat.

"Honey, what's wrong?"

"Bad dream, that's all. Nothing. Go back to sleep."

"That was no 'dream.' That was a nightmare to end nightmares. You were screaming and about to wake up the kids."

"It's okay…"

"No, Tom, it's not. This had to do with you and the Marines. We will not go back to sleep until you tell me what's up. Got it?"

Tom looked at his buxom, dark-skinned wife and saw that look in her eyes that said he had better do what she wanted, or there would be no sleep tonight. He sighed, then took her in his arms.

"I saw a ghost today. Or at least someone who should be a ghost."

"At the cemetery?"

"Yes. At a grave I had no idea was there."

"Whose grave was it?"

"Corporal Mike Muller. The Marine who kept me from dying."

Tom asked Julie Stindel to meet him the next morning before he picked up the six teenagers. He handed her two names and identifiers he could find.

"You still have contacts through the Recruiters?"

"Yes, Tom. But you say Muller is dead. What about this, uh, David Krewson?"

"I thought he was dead also. He is alive and walking around but not in good shape. I need to try and work some things out for both Marines."

Julie knew some of the stories as to how Tom had a partial disability from his time in the Sandbox. Like many a Veteran, he kept a lot inside. It had been her experience that the more a person had done or seen, the less they talked about it.

"Okay. I'll work on it. Those kids driving you nuts yet?"

Tom laughed. "I've been a bit nuts for years. They can't make it any worse."

Tom and the six teenagers were back at Evergreen Cemetery at 9:00 AM. He unloaded all the tools and trash bags they would need, then walked them back to the Veteran's graves. Tom stopped them before they went through the beat-up metal archway entrance.

"Lookit. I told you all at the start of this detail that we will respect the dead. This is even more important as some of the people buried here died for something, not just of old age. They died defending their buddies next to them, fighting for what they think the country stands for, not to mention the freedoms of others. So please, a little reverence to those who often went the extra mile for their fellow humans." Tom stood for a few moments, then spoke again. "Speech over. Time to work."

Partway through the morning, Tim approached him. "Can I talk to you alone?"

"Go ahead. Walk with me for a moment."

As they walked, the jock began to talk. "We moved around a lot while my Dad was in the military. He was a USAF pilot, thought he had a chance at a General's slot."

Tom remained quiet, knew the young man would continue as he could.

"He started drinking, then whoring around when he was overseas. Some people noticed, and he was told that was it, start looking for a retirement station. That was when he started beating on my mom when we lived off base. I was twelve."

"That made you grow up fast," Tom said.

"Yeah. And my mom's side of the family, the men are large. So I got my growth early, and sports were easy for me. Then one day, my dad hit my mom one too many times." Tim paused and looked at Tom.

"I beat the holy shit out of him. That was the end of any father-son stuff."

"Sometimes, PTSD can cause people to do some bad things. That is not an excuse, Tim, just a reason."

"He flew some combat missions, but not as many as most. Nah, he just began to use the bottle as a crutch."

Tom stopped and looked at the young man. "And you? You going to start drinking?"

"Been there, done that, Sir. I plan on going to Family of Alcoholics Anonymous meetings here soon. That is if I can work off the beef that got me here cleaning graves."

"A drunken brawl when you are underage is not a good idea."

"Yes. Got kicked out of sports until I graduate. I just want to say I didn't mean to disrespect the guys you served with just because my dad was an asshole."

"Here, Son. Shake. We all make mistakes, wave our pricks around."

"That homeless guy, you knew him from before."

"Yep. And I hope to be able to explain to you and the others the whole story. Now, back to work. This area needs a whole lot of TLC."

The group worked until lunch, then went back to the van. Tom had added some fried chicken and potato salad to the meal. The hopeful graduates loosened up and began to share life stories. Tim had already told everyone about his misadventure with booze and fighting.

The Wheeler Brothers soon explained what they did to warrant a second chance work detail instead of Juvie Hall.

"See, there was this cherry BMW at our dad's shop. So Mack and I took it for a spin."

Mack began to laugh. "Then the cops started chasing us—it was three o'clock in the morning and we were going over a hundred twenty miles an hour."

"Yeah, they couldn't keep up. But then Mack here wrecked it."

"You think you can do any better, Mike? Just because you're nine months older than me doesn't make you any smarter."

"What did your dad do?" Asked Tom.

"Took a hickory switch to us."

"No, you didn't! " Megan burst out. "You did not get beat by a switch! You did not grow up in the Deep South. You and this phony redneck crap is getting on our nerves."

Mike smirked.

"At least we weren't nekkid when we were caught in the car."

Susie stood up.

"I swear to God I'm going to kick your butts."

"No, sorry," said Tom. "No physical violence."

"Why were you naked?" Nick interjected.

"You don't have to talk about that if you don't want to, young ladies," said Tom.

Susie and Megan looked at each other. Then Megan spoke. "Okay. So this is like an AA meeting where we all share. Here goes." Megan took a deep breath and let it out.

"We are best friends. After raiding Suzie's parents' liquor cabinet, we decided to borrow her Aunt's car and go somewhere private to, you know…"

The males all stared at her, waiting for the complete answer.

"Okay. We were bi-curious. We wanted to see if we like women better than men."

"Do you?" asked Nick.

"None of your goddamned business, you voyeur prick!"

Everyone laughed. Tom finally stepped in to gain some control again.

"Okay. Enough sex stuff. I do not want to get in hot water over sexual harassment."

"What about *your* story, big mouth Nick?" demanded Susie. Nick shrugged.

"Stabbed a guy with a pencil for dissing my sister and mother."

"That doesn't sound like much."

"Took his eye out. Wanted to kill him."

Everyone was silent. Nick continued.

"Maybe I ain't a real Mafiosa or know any of them. But with my people, my family, we still don't allow people to disrespect our mothers and sisters. So, here I am. My legal advisor got them to recognize it as an accident."

"And you just said otherwise," Tom said.

"Hey, confession is good for the soul."

Tom looked at the six students hoping to graduate. They had just shared their serious mistakes, were realizing they had to work to overcome them, but at least they were willing to try to better themselves.

"How about you, Mister Washington?" asked Susie. "Any sharing?"

He smiled, then spoke. "I'll just say that where I lived, there were still judges and lawyers willing to allow malcontents to join the military instead of going to jail."

"What about that homeless guy. You knew him, right?"

"That is a story still in progress. Hopefully, I'll be able to share the complete tale someday soon. Now, back to work."

A month before graduation, there was a sudden special school assembly scheduled. No one knew what it was all about, just that there was supposed to be a special guest or two.

The Six (as the cemetery group called themselves) had what is referred to as a bonding experience, and all became friends. They often hung out together, joking about what had happened during the Evergreen Cemetery Cleanup. Tom Washington told them it was similar to Boot Camp bonding. People from entirely different backgrounds who would never consider being friendly with each other did form a bond over a collective stressful experience.

"You just had to face up to your screw-ups while cleaning up used condoms and feces, human and otherwise," Tom had said. "Not as dangerous or stressful as military training with live ammunition, but still not for the faint-hearted."

Nick demonstrated an artistic talent few knew he had when he designed a particular patch for them. It was a tombstone with a big blood-red '6' on it, with their first names after the words "Here Lies." Tom had demanded a patch also, and Nick made him one in the form of a chrome chain. The Former Marine's wife thought he was nuts to use it, but she knew it meant something. Jenine would soon learn the depth of the experience.

When the word spread that Tom Washington was

there, the Six knew something was up. Thus, they made it a point to sit together. Vice Principal Julia Stindel walked onto the stage of the sizable combination theater and conference auditorium, and there were gasps and 'What the' heard about the student body. She was in her full Marine Corps Gunnery Sergeant Dress Uniform, some students not knowing she was a Veteran, and few knew she had been a Marine. She called the assembly to order and began to explain the event.

"A large portion of you are nearing graduation. Others wish it was nearer for you." This elicited some light laughter from the student body and teachers.

"When you leave high school, you will be on to bigger and better things. That is, once you figure out what you want to do with the rest of your life."

Julia paused for a few moments and then continued.

"I faced the same decision making and joined the Marine Corps. I wanted to do something different than the rest of my family. In doing so, I was sent to dangerous places and met both bad and good people. It helped in my decision to become an educator, a teacher, as I knew that there would always be teenagers trying to become functioning adults. If you saw some of the youngsters in foreign lands being suckered into becoming suicide bombers, then you would understand how I never wanted any of you to have to face that decision."

"But today is not about me. It is about a couple of other Marines, one some of you have gotten to know, and one who was in our midst, but no one knew."

There was some murmuring in the audience as students tried to figure out what she was talking about.

"First, let me introduce former Marine Staff Sergeant Thomas Washington. Some of you know him quite well."

Tom walked onto the stage in his full dress uniform also, having to obtain some tailoring to get his beefy frame into his old accouterments.

"Thank You, Principal Stindel." Tom turned and

looked at the assembly and began speaking.

"I had the distinct pleasure of working with a few of your fellow students in less than pleasurable circumstances, not that long ago." There were a few titters from people who knew the details of his statement as Tom continued.

"While we were working cleaning up the local Evergreen Cemetery, I had a chance to visit the Veterans section, where military members who died now rest. And there I met someone I thought was long since dead. I believed at first I was looking at a ghost, being in a cemetery with graves about. But when he called me by name, I knew he was flesh and blood."

Tom looked offstage and smiled.

"For it was Corporal David Krewson, who is here to tell you an extraordinary true story about a Marine whose gravesite is in Evergreen Cemetery, unbeknown to most everyone, including those who he saved. Now without further adieu, let me present Corporal Krewson to tell the story.

"Holy shit," whispered Susie, "it's the homeless guy!"

A once filthy with tangled hair homeless man was now a very Strac Marine in dress uniform to match the others. He had filled out some thanks to some better health care and better food. But he still had streaks of gray in his dark hair. He walked up to Tom, shook hands, then hugged him. There was some applause that Krewson quickly signed to end it.

"Ladies and Gentlemen, this is not about me. This is about the man in the grave some of you cleaned up. And a nice job you did."

David Krewson looked at the Six and smiled. Then he continued.

"This is about teaching attributed to Jesus Christ. Whether you are a Christian or not, what he said holds true in my estimation. 'Greater love hath no man than this, that a man lay down his life for his friends.' It is recorded that Jesus said this not long before his seizure, knowing full well the torture and death he was about to face."

"I am here to put truth into that statement by telling the story of how a Marine, one Private First Class Michael Muller, did just that. He demonstrated that love and gave his life so that Tom and I are here today."

As David began to tell the tale of PFC Muller, memories flashed through Tom's mind as if it had all happened yesterday...

Their unit was on checkpoint duties on some main road running through some shithole of a village in the Sandbox. They were operating it with indigenous Military members, soldiers from the supposedly allied government. Tom and the others knew the some of the local populace was far from friendly to U.S. Forces, and with a language barrier, it made matters worse. In this environment came one Michael Muller, Private First Class from the backwoods of Washington State.

Muller was always a happy go lucky type who seemed not to be upset by much. Some of his fellow Marines nicknamed him 'Goofy' because of his demeanor as well as his unique laugh. Muller took this all in stride, smiled when people called him Goofy and kidded them right back. He was always on time, never tried to back out of an assignment, was ready to respond to a call for help.

The checkpoint had been built up into a more permanent affair by the construction of large cement barricades as well as a bollard or two. Vehicles and people approaching had to wind their way through a short serpentine path until they arrived at the guard shack, a two-room structure reinforced with sandbags for blast and shrapnel protection.

Tom had been the ranking NCO on duty that day, with David, one of his fireteam leaders. Muller was a member of David's fireteam. As vehicles and people came and went, the Marines rotated as to who was on point with an indigenous language speaker and who was in a support position. Nothing of any real importance or threat had occurred for days on end.

The Marines were settling in for a month of boredom before being rotated.

Then it happened.

It was Monday morning, some 8:00 AM local time when an individual in the local military uniform approached on foot. The local army units were sloppy about notifying the Marines when they had a change in personnel, people needed to be relived, and so forth. Thus a lone figure in uniform walking up was no big deal. However, something about this individual caught Muller's eye. No one would ever know what he saw as he would not be alive long enough to tell.

"Hey, Buddy, what's up?" Muller said as he suddenly walked towards the man. Tom looked towards Muller and David took a step in Muller's direction. Then it happened.

Michale Muller yelled, "Bomb!" and threw himself on to the figure just a yard away. Holding on to the subject, Michael Muller propelled them to between two of the thick cement barricades.

Authorities could never figure out how the enemy had packed so much explosive onto one persons body, but the Green on Blue attack was devastating. The cement barricades were ravaged, Tom and David were both knocked flat by the blast. Shrapnel hit Marines and civilians alike. One thing was definitely discovered during the After Action Investigation. By propelling the suicide bomber in between the two cement barricades, the only fatalities were Muller and the attacker.

Very little of Muller was recovered by Graves and Registration for burial. Tom, David and some others wound up spending time in the hospital. It took months for the ringing in Tom's ears to go away. He was eventually medically retired as he had received some other wounds on previous deployments.

David never got rid of the ringing in his ears. He rotated out with disability and disappeared.

"I survived in body thanks to Michael Muller," continued David Krewson, "but not in spirit. For I thought, 'why him and not me?' How did I survive and this happy guy nicknamed Goofy was blown to smithereens while trying to save us all? Experts call it survivors guilt."

The Corporal paused, then continued. "I came back to the U.S. and proceeded to self-destruct. Things became a blur. Some of you—" he looked at the Six, "—saw me at my worse."

"Then I found that grave by pure chance. And then Tom here found me."

"What are the chances two survivors from that day would suddenly be drawn to the person's grave who saved us, sacrificed his life for us? One in a million?"

David looked out at the assembly and noticed some tears. "I think Mike Muller's love reached out so that we would meet again. So that Tom here, also a friend, would help drag me up so I could function again. For that is what brotherly and sisterly love is about. Help and sacrifice. Please take that with you in your journey into the world.

"Now, if I may ask. A moment of silence for the late Michale Muller. For without his sacrificial love, I would not be here."

After the assembly, students and teachers came up to David Krewson to share, hug, and thank him for coming there. Tom snuck back into the shadows as he did not want the story to become about him. It should be about David and Michael.

"So, trying to hide, Mister Washington?"

The voice was young Megan's. Standing near her was the rest of the Six. Tom smiled as he asked, "Ready for graduation? You all are graduating, right?"

"Thanks to you, yes," said Mike Wheeler.

"Hey, you all put in the time, the work, worked on righting your mistakes, not me."

"Vice Principal Stindel told us you didn't have to take

us on, but you did," said Tim. "Can we all stay in touch? Or is that against the rules."

Tom grinned.

"I don't know why you would want to keep in touch with an old former Marine, but yes, you can."

"We want to stay in touch because you sacrificed for us. Showed us some love and caring," said Susie. "That is hard for non-family sometimes. It's hard for family also."

"Now, you are going to get me all teary-eyed. Don't you know you are not supposed to see Marines cry."

"But you do," interjected Nick. "You did for your buddies who died."

Tom paused, then answered.

"Yes, I did."

"You're coming to Graduation, right?" asked Mack Wheeler. "We'll give you a ride."

Tom laughed. "In a hot car? Newly stolen? No way!"

The Six laughed, then, before Tom could protest, pulled him into a group hug. As they parted, Tom held up the keychain Nick had made. Attached were some military dog tags. "This will be one of my many treasures as time goes by."

"Are those your dog tags?" asked Megan.

"Mine, and reproductions of Muller's, and a copy of David's."

"Why?"

"To remind me what Jesus said about sacrificial love. And my friends."

Tom left the Six at the school. When he arrived home, his wife and children were waiting.

"Hey, what's up?"

"Early Father's Day. We have your favorite dinner ready, the kids say they will stay home and do anything you want."

"Why?" Asked Tom.

"Sometimes, you need to sacrifice something for the

ones you love. Even if it is just time and effort."

The former Marine smiled.

"So true. So very true."

Falling for Grace
Elaina Gonzales-Blanton

In the Beginning

I don't have a name yet, or a body. I am a soul in Heaven and I was just born out of a star. I don't remember being born. I am just here and I am here with other beings and stars. Then there are our teachers, the angels and God. We are made of what God calls "energy and light" and because we are born of stars, when you look up at your earthly sky at night, you will see us. Though, to you, we look like bright big stars. When our earthly bodies die we come back to heaven and we can choose to stay here and teach, or go back to earth. God lets us choose.

None of us understand how God creates us. We just know that one minute we are here and then we exist forever—be it in a body on earth or in heaven. We are told that God creates a brand new soul whenever a human does something good for the world, but nobody really knows why God makes us. We are told that all new souls start out first in heaven with the other souls, angels and God, and then we learn about earth and the kinds of bodies that we can choose to be born into.

We also do a great bit of learning from the souls that have returned from earth whose earthly bodies have died as they have fresh knowledge to give. We can choose to be born into whatever kind of being, or body that we want to, and we decide when we are ready to go to earth. Some souls immediately decide to go to heaven, others like me take our time and learn about the world. Although here in heaven among the stars, time is much different. Time isn't in minutes or hours, time is whatever we chose to make it. And so, with our "time," we watch people and animals from our heavenly windows into the earth, and we study the behaviors and then if we want to, we discuss our desires with God, and then we get born on earth. I have decided that I want to go to earth, but I am unsure of which kind of being that I want to be.

From what I have observed of humanity, humans can be very cruel and I want to be sure that whatever being I am born into is good for the world. My next step is to have the conversation with God and decide who I will be and I am on my way to see God to do just that.

God is sitting on the sun, as I approach.

I say, "God, I want to be born on earth but I don't know as what. Do you have any suggestions, or is there a particular need?"

God replies, "Child of mine, there is always a need but I will tell you that earth can always use more of one very special being. Earth can always use more dogs."

"A dog? As I have observed, I know that dogs are loyal, protective and seem to love their humans no matter how badly they treat them, and there seems to be an abundance of dogs on earth. I can't imagine that there is a shortage, or even why a soul would want to be a dog because many are abused and abandoned. Why a dog?" I ask earnestly.

"There is no such thing as an abundance of dogs, or

any beings. Once you are on earth, you will understand this. As far as why a soul would want to be a dog-again, once you are born, this will all become more clear to you. You are here to learn, and you go to earth to experience. Experiences are what truly teaches us. It is true that humanity is flawed and can be cruel, and so can animals. If you observe animals in the wild, you will see this. Every soul ever created has a purpose either here, or on earth. Humans often fret over things such as eating animals and killing bugs and it is unnecessary. I do not put a hierarchy on life, people do. You would serve a fine purpose to go to earth as a dog because dogs are the best friends of humans, and the protectors of the human heart, and sometimes dogs save the lives of humans. There is a woman on earth who is suffering greatly and she needs help, and I think that you are the perfect soul to help her. Will you do it?"

I nod. "Yes, I will do it. Is there anything more that I should know before I go to earth?"

"It will be a very intense beginning for you, but know that I am with you and that you are there because you are needed."

I take a breath. "Okay, I'm ready."

Grace

Well, let's see. I am in a body. At least I think I am but there is no light. It's dark, not like heaven where there is all light and everything feels good. I knew it wouldn't be like heaven but this is so dark, and I think I am cold. This body I am in is doing weird things and moving uncontrollably. Okay, let me try to think and remember what I saw from watching dogs on earth.

Oh yes, I have this stuff that humans call fur, and I

have a tail, and that thing I am feeling must be my body telling me to eat. Or maybe I need warmth. I just can't see anything. I'm going to try to figure out this dog body but I'm so confused. There is something happening. I think I am being touched by another dog.

Yes, I am being touched by another dog. This dog is doing things to me and I don't like it. I just made a noise and I don't know how I did it. I think I just cried. This dog just grabbed me and got me feeling all weird. Maybe this is my dog mom or my dog dad?

I cry and yelp. I am confused and scared. *Where is God?*

My dog mom understands and assures me, "I am your mom and you are safe. I was kissing you. You need to eat now and I will show you how to do that. I love you, my precious baby."

My dog dad tells me, "I am your dad, and you are one of our daughters. Mom will feed you and I will help her to teach you, your brothers and sisters how to be a dog. I love you, my beautiful daughter."

Three Weeks Later

I am running around, and playing with other dogs and my siblings, and I am told that I poop and pee a lot too. I really like eating because I eat from my mom's body and it means that I get to be close to her, and so I eat a lot, even if I am not really hungry. I really like being with my mom. I also like to use my teeth and chew on my dog mom and dog dad, and dog brothers and sisters, but they chew on me back and I don't like that and so I cry to make them stop. Dog dad lets me chew on him more than dog mom does. Dog dad also chases me and lets me chase him back.

I have met humans and they are very kind to me. They like to hold me. They tell me that I am "cute" and I think that is a good thing. They call me "Chunky Butt Grace." They tell me that I am a "German Shepherd puppy and a Big Girl." There are other earthly beings here, one in particular that seems like it might be a dog, but it is mean to me and the other dogs and tries to hit us when we come up to it. This creature has an odd shaped head, and does not smell good at all. Its butt has an especially offensive smell. It also does not bark. Instead, it makes other noises that hurt my ears.

Mom and dad call this thing a "cat" and I have some memories from heaven of having observed a cat and I think it would be wise to stay away from this cat. Dog mom and dad tell me that we live with a "breeder" and that this means that they make special puppies for humans to love.

Three More Weeks Later

I am eating even more, but not from my dog mom, from a bowl. I no longer get my mother's milk. This food in the bowl is sometimes soft and wet, sometimes hard and dry but it tastes really good. I miss eating from my dog mom but I really like my new food and my bowl. I am pooping and peeing a lot more and I get to do that outside, and I like going outside. I like to run and chase all the other creatures including the humans. I am told to "not chase the cat" even though the cat growls at me and makes other noises that make me think he wants to hurt me.

Dog mom and dad say that the cat is a "jerk." I like to bark, a lot, especially at the jerk cat! I really like it when the humans throw balls at me, but I don't like bringing them back as they demand. If you throw a ball at me, it is mine. If you don't throw a ball at me, the ball is mine. All off the balls are mine and the humans have not learned that yet. I have met some humans that I am told will be "taking me home soon." My mom tells me that I will be going to be with my human mom. I want to stay with my dog mom and dog dad and these "breeder" humans.

Most of my brothers and sisters have all left us to be with their new humans, and I don't like it. I don't remember much of what it was like in heaven, and I wish that I did. I do like it here on earth though. Every human that I meet seems to like me and think I am cute. They tell me that I have a "big, fluffy tail, beautiful German Shepherd markings, and big puppy dog eyes." I am still called "Chunky Butt Grace" and the humans laugh when they say my name. My dog mom is called "Jade," my dog dad is "Jasper," and nobody laughs when say their names. I am told that my new human family will change my name. I am okay with that because I think that "Chunky Butt" is a baby name and like my humans tell me, I am a "Big Girl."

I just went to a place where there was a human called a "veterinarian." I did not like it there. They hurt me. They put things in me that felt like I was being bitten and they put something up my butt! That "veterinarian" is a jerk, just like that cat and I didn't just bark at that veterinarian, I bit him too! After I bit the veterinarian, they wrapped me up really tight and I couldn't move and they did more pokes and bites and then I finally was done. Dog mom and dad told me that I have to go back again for more bites. We'll see about that.

Two Weeks Later

I went back to the veterinarian and they bit me again, a bunch more times and it hurt so much! I didn't get to bite back this time because they wrapped me up before I got a chance. The veterinarian says that I am "ready to get adopted," whatever that means. I have a bad feeling.

One Week Later

I kissed my dog mom and dad goodbye, I kissed my breeder humans good bye, I knocked over the cat with my butt, and then the new humans took me. I don't like these humans. I don't know why but I just don't like them and I growled at the human man when he picked me up. He didn't do anything to me but I was ready to bite if he was mean to me because he seems like he could be mean. The human woman stinks but not a good stink that makes me want to eat her or lick her. She doesn't smell like dog butt or a piece of steak. She smells like... she smells like she's been rolling in cats! What did I just get into?

Three Days Later

These new humans have a lot of cats. There are cats in every room and the cats hurt me. They hit me with their paws and take my food from me. I don't have any balls or sticks to play with. There is a little human here that calls me "baby" but the big humans call me "stupid." I think that these humans are sick or confused because I don't know if my name is baby or stupid and I don't think that they know either. I do not have a big yard like I did with my breeder humans. There only rooms here and I am made to pee and poop on a big piece of paper. The first time I peed and I didn't know I was supposed to pee on the paper and the human man hit me in the face. I growled at him and he hit me again and so I ran and hid under a bed.

One Week Later

The little human makes me sleep in bed with her and still calls me baby. I like her. She kisses me and holds me. I do not like that she makes me sleep with her, but I will allow it since she is a little human. I think she is scared of her man human, who I think is her dad. He hits her like he did me, only it's not for peeing in the wrong place. He hits her for doing a lot of things. The man also hits the human woman. I want to bite this man where he pees but I don't want to get kicked. He kicked me the other day when I growled at one of the cats. It hurt, so I won't do that again. I try to hide when I am not being held by the little human. I am very hungry, because the humans do not let me eat a lot. I am starting to think that coming to earth was not a wise choice.

God told me that a woman needed me, but this woman doesn't even talk to me or play with me. The child seems to need me, but she is not a woman, and God said "woman," so I am confused. I do not like it here. I am afraid of the man, and they seem to really like the cats, but not me, and I don't know why. Maybe I am bad at being a dog. Maybe I poop too much. I am not a smart dogs like the dogs I observed from heaven. I know this because the man still calls me stupid.

Two Weeks Later

The little human and the woman are not in the house anymore. Today some humans that I have never seen before came over and they were very big, and strong humans and they took the little human girl away with them. The human woman left after the little human girl was taken. I miss the girl. She was the only one that liked me and the only one that fed me. I wish that the big, strong humans would have taken me with the girl. The human man is here and he stinks of something I've not smelled before. He is drinking something that does not look like water out of big containers and he tried to make me drink it too, but it came back up out of me. He hit me when the stuff that is not water came back out of me.

This man is so bad. He is a very, very bad man. I don't know why I was born anymore. I should have stayed in Heaven. I think that God lied to me about dogs being human's best friend. I don't have any friends since the little human girl got taken. I would try to be friends with the cats but they don't like me and try to hurt me every time I walk by them.

One Week Later

The cats hurt me very bad. They all came at me, and hit me with their paws and cut me open and liquid came out of me. I bit a cat and the human man threw me against the wall. I am okay, but I hate this place.

The Next Day

The human man is taking me somewhere in his box that moves. It is very cold out, and I am shaking but at least I am outside. It is dark but I can see that we have come to a park! Yes, we are at a park! Oh, I hope that this human man has started to like me. Maybe he will play ball with me. If he does, I will let him have the ball and we can share it. There are no other humans here that I can see and there are no dogs, either. Maybe the human man wants to play with me and only me.

He just hit me in my head, and threw me out of his box that moves, and he left. I am cold and hungry in this dark park, and I am all alone. Nobody loves me. I am stupid.

Gabby

My face is black and blue and my eye is throbbing so hard it feels like it will explode out of my head. My ear is ringing and my head is pounding. All I hear are the words: "stupid bitch." That's what Mike calls me. Mike is my husband. My name is actually Gabriella, or Gabby for short, but for the last two years, my name has been Stupid Bitch.

I married Mike twenty-three months ago and he hit me for the first time the day after our honeymoon. He said that I was giving my dog Annabelle more attention than him. I wasn't. I was just cuddling with her after having spent a week away from her with him in Mexico. Annabelle has been my best friend for many years and Mike seemed to love her up until that day when he of the blue grabbed me by my hair, pulled me off the couch and told me that if I didn't put the dog in her kennel he would hit her.

Annabelle, a large German Shepherd, is very protective of me and she growled at Mike. He then grabbed her by her neck and shoved her into her kennel. Annabelle barked and growled for hours and Mike hit and kicked me over and over until I passed out that night. I woke up to Annabelle asleep in her kennel, and Mike told me he had given her some meat with valium in it. He drugged my dog.

I dated this man for over a year before I married him and he had no problem with her, but now he hates her so much that I can't even spend time with her without him hitting or kicking us both. I quit my job as a social worker to move across the state to be with him and I have nobody here but this man and my dog. Both of my parents are dead and I have no siblings so Mike is my family. Mike and I had decided that I would stay home while we tried to have a baby, and I quit taking birth control so that I could get pregnant. But after he hit me the first time I knew that I had made a big mistake and so when Mike was at work, I went to the local clinic and got the IUD because I knew that I cannot have a baby with him.

I hate myself. I am a stupid bitch, just like he says because I should know better than this. My best friend Tina stopped being my friend because she was mad at me for not leaving Mike the first time he hit me. She and I met while we were in college, and both working at a local battered women's shelter. I am an educated woman, and I had a job that I enjoyed and I made a good money at it, and I left it all for this man who is just like the men whom I have tried to save dozens of women from.

I've had over 120 hours of training in domestic violence victim advocacy and yet I cannot help or save myself. My body aches and my face and head pound. I've gone to my doctor for the pain and she asks me how I got hurt, and I lie to her and tell her that I fell.

After the third time I went in for falling, she wanted to do an MRI to see if I have something wrong with my brain or nervous system that is causing me to fall. I refused the MRI and she then said to me, "Gabby, are you really falling or is someone hurting you?"

I froze. I did not expect her to ask me this. Or maybe I did. Either way, her question made my throat get dry, and my stomach hurt. I couldn't speak. I wanted to tell her but all I could hear in my head was Mike saying to me, "If you tell anyone about me hurting you, I'll kill Annabelle." I finally spoke and told my doctor that I trip over the dog, and she said "okay" and let it go.

Mike came home from work and saw the print out from my doctor's office. The printout read, *Gabby age 32, presenting with bruises on torso and face, and head pain. Patient was asked if she were being hurt by someone intentionally and denies it. MRI is highly recommended as to determine cause of frequent falls however patient reports that she trips over her dog frequently.*

Mike knew that I had gone to see Dr. Stevens but he thought it was for a pregnancy test, because that's what I told him. The print out didn't say anything about a pregnancy test because I had forgotten to get one because I knew I wasn't pregnant. I had gone there for the pain from him hitting and kicking me and I did not think to tell Dr. Stevens to be vague in her notes and even if I had, she'd know I was being hurt and might have reported the abuse to the police. I am so dumb. I needed to have at least asked for a pregnancy test.

"Why didn't you get a pregnancy test, Gabby?"

"I did. She just must not have notated it."

"Why did the doctor ask about your bruises and why does it say that you went to her for pain?"

"I don't know, Mike. I guess maybe she saw my bruises."

"You went there to tell her that I beat you up, didn't you?"

"No, Mike, I did not! The paper even says that I denied being hurt by anyone."

"You think you're so smart because you went to college and you were a social worker, and I'm just a dumb construction worker, don't you, Gabby?!"

"No Mike, I don't."

His fist connecting to my face felt like I was hitting my head into a brick wall. I know what it feels like for my head to hit a brick wall because one time Mike slammed my head into the brick wall in our basement. He hit me again and again until I passed out. I woke up to the sound of Annabelle yelping.

I got up from the floor and saw Mike covered in blood with a big gash on his arm and Annabelle tearing at him with her claws and teeth. She had pulled him off of me, and now he was the one that was crying for help. I tried to get up to get to them but I couldn't walk straight. Mike's phone was laying on the table and I crawled over to it to call 911. I couldn't call the other times because Mike had always had his phone on him and he had taken mine away from me and broken it.

And so I called 911 and told the operator that my husband was beating me and my dog was attacking him, and then I heard another yelp from Annabelle. I looked over and she was on the floor, not moving and no longer biting Mike. I dropped the phone and screamed her name and she didn't look at me. Her eyes were blank and she was still. I screamed at Mike, "*What did you do to her?!*"

"I broke that dumb dog's neck!"

When I heard those words I felt a pain in my body that was worse than any pain I have ever felt, even when being beaten by Mike and then I passed out. I woke up in the hospital a few hours later. I stayed in the hospital for a week with a concussion and Mike was arrested and is in jail awaiting court for charges of domestic violence and animal cruelty. The policeman that came to talk to me in the hospital told me that even though Mike had killed Annabelle because she had been attacking him he was being charged because she had attacked him to save my life.

So now here I am, I don't have my dog, or my best

friend or my husband. I do have my freedom but that came at a cost to the one soul that truly loved me. I don't want to do this anymore. Losing Annabelle was too much. I am going to take these pain pills that the hospital gave me and I am going to die.

Grace

Oh, what's that? I think I smell a human woman. I'm going to follow this smell. Oh, it is a human, a human woman! There is a human woman in this park! Yes, I am not alone! Oh, but she probably won't want to be my friend. Maybe I shouldn't go up to her. Oh no, she is coming over to me. What if she hits me too? I am scared. She is talking to me in a kind voice that makes me want to come to her and she is saying "come here, puppy." But I don't know about this. She does smell differently that the human man who hurt me and the human woman that left when the little girl human was taken. I will go up to her.

The human woman let me smell her hand first, and then she picked me up, is now holding me tight like the little human girl used to. She has put me inside of her blanket that she wears. Her face is wet and I think that she is sad like I am sad, because water is coming out of her eyes, and so I will kiss her and try to make her happy. She kisses me back.

Gabby

Hi puppy. Who are you? Let me see your collar. Oh I see, it says that your name is Grace. I saw the man hurt you and leave you here. I don't know why someone would do that to you, but I am so sorry, and I know how it feels to be hurt. You are a German Shepherd puppy. I used to have a German Shepherd. Her name was Annabelle. I had her for twelve years, but she died not long ago and she died because of me. She was all that I had and I miss her so much that I came here tonight to die. But you know what, Grace? I'm not so sure about that now. I really do not know what to think now. What am I going to do with you? You are just a baby and I can't leave you out here all alone with it being so dark and cold. But then I didn't come here with plans on walking out. I came here to take this bottle of pills and die with the peacefulness of the darkness and the cold, but it's not so peaceful here anymore with you whining and licking me."

Grace

I am kissing this human woman all over and I am wagging my tail and climbing on her, because I do not want her to leave me, or to die. I do not want the sadness in her anymore. I am going to kiss her and wag my tail until the sadness is all gone! Oh my goodness, her eyes are still watering. I must make them stop. I put kisses all over this human. I really like this human.

Please God, make her want to not die and make her want to be my human. Please God. I am not going to stop kissing you, human woman, not until you stop making the water come out of your eyes! I am going to shake my butt at you now and wag may tail in your face! Come on, human woman! Come on, stop being sad! You know what, human woman? I *love* you, you are my new mom, so you can't die now! Come on now and love me back. You know that you want to! I am barking at her now.

"Human woman! Human woman! *I love you, human woman!* You are *my* human! Human woman, stop making the water come out of your face or I will lick it all up! I am going to chew on this blanket that you wear."

Gabby

Okay, okay, okay, wow! You are a very kissy puppy Mrs. Grace! Oh, now you want to chew on me?" I laugh. "Okay, I like you too. I like your big brown puppy eyes and your wiggly butt, and your wagging tail, and you are so darn soft. I think that maybe Annabelle sent you because just five minutes ago I didn't have a reason to live and now, now I have you."

"Let's go live, Grace. Let's go live."

MOVING ON
Eliza Loeb

She wanted to say how much the music sucked without sounding overly critical of another persons taste. The scene of the club just wasn't something she really felt capable of fitting in to, and more or less stuck out like a sore thumb.

Alas, such was the nature of block parties and festivals on Seattle's Capital hill. College students from UW and CSU would traipse about, dancing to a flurry of music in clubs that did not require membership to access. Privileged children who barely lifted a finger would drink their feelings away in a wave of cheap beer and dollar shelf liquor and someone would be crying over their partner for only glancing at another human being and call it cheating. And to add insult to injury, Felicity Hartford's date had merely repeated everything that she had been thinking about with a great deal of disdain for those who lacked the time or tolerance for such trivial endeavors.

"I mean, really…" the woman with her said. "Just who the hell acts that high and mighty to a point where they think it's ok to look down on normal people for having fun?"

Felicity gave the girl a cool smile and said nothing as

she continued on with her rant. Arguing with her would prove futile and if anything, she would likely just get a free meal at the end of the day and call it good. Her eyes traveled down to her reflection in her drink as she listened to every little quip and foul remark her date had made, going into politics and how trans folks were only trans because they wanted attention, eventually going on about how bi- or pansexuality among POC communities were just a means to push a political agenda. By that point, Felicity downed the last of her beverage and stood to retrieve her wallet and called for the cheque.

"What's wrong?" the woman asked.

Once again, Felicity didn't answer. Instead, she placed her credit card in the receipt folder and passed it back to the server before standing and turning to leave.

"I-is it something I said?" The woman sounded panicked at this point and proceeded to chase her out of the restaurant, touching her shoulder. "If it is, I am really sorry!"

Felicity turned around and frowned at her now former date and rolled her eyes. "Do you really mean that, or are you saying that so I will go inside and continue to tolerate you?"

From the look on the woman's face, Felicity could see how much her words stung. Yet sometimes, people would give knee jerk reactions of the same coin when they know that they've been caught or when they know that they aren't capable of controlling another individual who they feel might fuel their own self deluded egos.

"You don't even know me," the woman sobbed.

All the other woman could do was give a cold and unfeeling stare to their date and shrug them off. The beginning of the date had gone well. Felicity had been trying to step out of her comfort zone to see how this potential partner ticked. See how she would match.

She was beautiful to boot, with her red Louboutins, her khaki pencil skirt, and teal turtle neck. And Felicity wouldn't deny that she was half expecting her date to be at least a little high maintenance and prissy to some degree. But when she opened her mouth, everything she had said rose red flags and began to rub Felicity the wrong way. And as everything that the woman had said came to mind, the more jaded of the two gave a low sigh.

"Listen," she began. "You would make great company for someone else who isn't me."

The woman paused. "What the hell is that supposed to mean?"

"It means that we aren't a good match."

"Bullshit, we aren't!" the woman snapped. "Opposites are *supposed* to attract!"

Felicity stared her up and down and pinched her brows together in frustration as the other woman loomed over her. To think that she had to go through this sort of thing with men most of the time and to finally run in to a woman who pulled the same bullshit had proven to be tiresome.

"But have you considered that maybe certain types of people *don't*?" she asked.

The other woman huffed and balled her fists, bordering on throwing an adult temper tantrum. And the longer Felicity stood where she was, the longer that she gave this person her time and the light of day meant the more control that the woman would have over her.

"I paid the bill," Felicity said, now with obvious contempt. "Please delete my number and don't contact me again."

"I'm your ride home!"

"I can take the bus."

"You can't just leave me alone...."

"I just did."

The way home would take a little longer than normal as she wondered around the city and back to Capital Hill. Her mind briefly described the metropolis's slowly crumbling infrastructure and how hollow relics of the past were finally being knocked down to make way for new condominiums and high rise apartments that only trust fund babies could afford. And as the days past, they would not deny that Seattle was becoming a hollow shell of what it used to be. Its citizens had been getting driven out by the day while rent continued to rise to near impossible heights.

The University District was getting to a point where it was almost unliveable for its students and fifteen an hour could barely afford a jug of milk and the cost of living. The homeless population had continued to rise to near unmanageable numbers and the city council and government continued to turn a blind eye. All because keeping people in an endless cycle of poverty and refusing to provide basic human needs meant keeping their pockets lined with cash that they hadn't even needed. And the very thought that the well-to-do continued to make comments like Felicity's nightmare of a date had set her on edge.

She grit her teeth at people like that.

She grit her teeth at being powerless to stop people like that.

"You seem troubled," came a voice.

A man with dark hair sat at a nearby gazebo as he sipped away at an appletini, watching her as she paced to and fro like some small animal in a burning cage. His expression was calm, if not amused and he had been leaning back and watching her as though her actions had been the stuff of decent daytime television. She, on the otherhand, remained unamused and still on edge from her previous interaction. She ignored him and walked on.

She had enough with dealing with potential obnoxious first dates and cared little for more boasts from pretentious douche bags who thought themselves—

She stopped as she passed by another dive bar. The same man from earlier had been sitting on the gazebo and laughing at a statement from another individual who had just delivered a Sex on the Beach. His pale cheeks had been slightly flushed from his drinking and she could swear that his pointed ears twitched as she passed him...

Wait. *Pointed?*

She shook away the thought and figured that it might have been some form of plastic surgery, moving onward as she had passed another bar with the same man sitting outside of that gazebo. This time, he had been watching her expectantly. His golden grey eyes flickered in the dim light as he beckoned her with his middle and forefinger. This time, she approached and settled into a seat with immense apprehension. How did he manage to follow her so far into the middle of Seattle proper? How was it that he could flit from gazebo to gazebo without a trace and not break a sweat.

"Do you wish to talk about it?" he asked.

"Do I wish to talk about....what?"

"Anything." His lips pulled into a wicked grin as he leaned forward. Handsome as he was, Felicity couldn't help but feel something off about the way he looked. "The Moon, the sun, your awful date and the fact that despite my frequent and frustrating materializations, why it is you are still trying to deny what is in front of you?"

"Well as someone who has been homeless and has more or less figured out the workings of this city, it's pretty obvious."

"That you don't believe in magic?"

She paused. This man had just called out to her on the street and is now putting words in her mouth. She really hated things like that, and while she wanted to run, she honestly felt no reason to. Instead she leaned back and folded her arms and looked him in the eye. He was handsome, she would give him that. His high cheekbones and narrow face gave him a fae king visage. Although, given that he looked as though he were Japanese or Korean, she didn't want to toss around assumptions. He could have been Hispanic or Native American... maybe Pacific Islander. She looked to his ears and took another double take. They were pointed at the tip and were slightly longer than that of a normal humans ears and his eyes... well, his eyes were almost cat like in the way they stared back at her.

"So what if I don't?"

"Then that is entirely your perspective."

Her brow furrowed. "In the very least, we have that cleared up."

"Indeed," he cheered, clapping his hands together.

"You mentioned my date." She said lowly. "Just how long have you been watching me?"

"Not too long."

This man's answers were slowly beginning to infuriate her. Yet she persisted, anyway. She still didn't feel uncomfortable and she in the very least wanted to talk about her most recent experience, along with her discomfort and dislike of how the city treats its less wealthy citizens to a point where they are driven out. And paused to wait for his input or his opinion from time to time. He simply smiled and urged her on, keeping his attention on her with interest as he sipped at his cocktail and offered to buy something for her. Instead of accepting, she continued as he had wished. And once she had decided that she had been silent for too long, she wasn't sure what she should think about it. Was he making fun of her? Was he genuinely interested in what she had to say? Was he trying to process everything?

"May I be frank?" he finally asked.

She ordered a drink and nodded, finally averting her gaze to say that she was done.

"I think you invest yourself too much with people who aren't willing to invest with you."

She grit her teeth.

"Now, you and I both know that Carrie something or whomever you were with earlier was a narcissistic sociopath. And in many instances, she might have been able to fool anyone else that she was interested, but many people who have been around or have had relationships with someone like her, like you, would have been weary from the get go."

His expression was now serious. He was no longer the same man who was gazing upon Felicity with interest, but with concern and understanding. As if to say that he knew what she had gone through and that he understood why she was the way she had been.

"You have seen and experienced too much in your short lifetime to expect anything else. You've even had a rough five year patch with a man who didn't even bother with you until your attention was on someone else or when it was most convenient for him. You wanted love, but he wanted a toy and you have been having a difficult time processing the matter and trying to figure out how you feel about the who situation as it is while constantly running from it instead of facing it head on."

"How did you—"

"You told me."

She looked down at the table feeling as though she were some sort of scolded child. Everything this man had been telling her was true. Everything he had been referring to from the past three hours alone was true.

"Now... Felicity, was it?" he asked.

"Yes."

"First of all, I really appreciate you being patient with me." He paused as she gave him a slight smile and nodded. "Second, I feel that you need to take time to yourself and reevaluate what you want from a relationship. Establish boundaries not only with others, but also with yourself. What are you okay with? What do you like? What are you comfortable with sharing with others about yourself so that a date doesn't feel one-sided?"

"What if I want more than just one romantic relationship?"

"Well, then you need to work up to that after you work up to you."

It took a few more hours before Felicity felt herself settle into comfort and the two would continue to talk about everything, and then nothing. Where she was from, what he liked. She invested as much interest as he had and often times found herself flirting before she pulled herself back. She didn't want to open herself up to him too much and even if she did, he reassured her by touching her hand and smiling down at her.

The two eventually left the establishment where they first sat down with one and other, moving from one to the other without a hitch and eventually continued on to a private club known as The Mercury. Felicity slowly swayed to and fro in the line as pain by Boy Harsher could be heard from the inside. Her companion watched her and eventually swayed with her. The wave was almost hypnotic as the singer crooned the lyrics, inviting the listener to draw themselves further and further into the tempo.

It hadn't been until a pair of hands reached out and took her by the hips, pulling her close to them and grinding into her as her eyes snapped open. The next moments had become a blur and the man she had been in line with was then seen setting a reasonable distance between her and the other individual who had been touching her. He kept his back to other people who had been struggling to remove the assailant from the property as Felicity looked up at her presently protective companion.

"I'm sorry," she mourned. "I was too busy talking about myself and having a good time that I never asked your name."

He straightened himself and sighed, rolling his eyes jokingly as he shrugged. "It's not like you had a rough night or anything."

"I..."

The corner of his mouth quirked and he placed a hand on her shoulder. "Relax, Feli." he laughed. "You can call me Dion, if you would like."

Feli? She knew that they only met today, but was it really okay to go by nicknames? Either way, the honesty and reassurance had been a nice change.

After the two had gone in, the rest of the night began to fade. All that could be remembered was dancing and euphoria as she swayed and moved to the beat of the music. She eventually invited the man that she now knew as Dion onto the dance floor and moved with him. Their bodies moved in sync with the music as the two slowly melted into a drunken frenzy of sweat and endorphins, to which an outsider looking in would assume that the two were lovers bonding in the heat of the moment.

He made a gesture to her as if to request permission to touch her as she granted him passage by guiding his hands to her sides. She moved closer to him and wrapped her arms around his shoulders as the song changed. When last call came, she called a rideshare to take the two home and slowly guided him back to her room, locking the door as they entered so that her roommates wouldn't walk into something that they wouldn't want to see. His lips pressed into the crook of her neck as warm hands brushed her hair to the side. Fingers deftly fumbled at the buttons of his dress shirt and teeth grazed at the exposed flesh of her breasts. She gasped as he yanked her onto his lap and slid his fingers up her thigh and beneath the hem of her shirt.

He seemed to enjoy the way her chest rose and fell as each breath she drew grew heavier and heavier, spreading her legs so that she could straddle him with his other hand and grip at the base of her rear as he ground against her through the straining fabric of his slacks.

"Do you want this?" he growled into a low whisper. "I won't continue unless the feeling is mutual."

He could feel her nod her head.

Unfortunately, a nod wasn't enough. He needed verbal confirmation before anything more were to continue tonight. Dion stopped his ministrations outright and gently pressed her back, nudging Felicity to look him in the eye.

"I need you to *tell* me that you want this," he pressed. "I won't continue with just a nod."

"I want this," she rasped.

He sighed and smiled, moving to brush her hair to the side as he wrapped his arm around her waist. A gentle smile stretched along his lips as he brushed them against hers.

"Good girl."

The next hours to follow seemed as though they could never end as Felicity's fingers intertwined with Dion's. His ministrations were all but unrequited as they continued to go back and forth with an endless array of heat and passion that it lasted well into the next afternoon for either to fall into a state of exhaustion. However, the confusion of whether last night had served to be a one night stand or not had remained to be seen. Would the two go on an official date after they woke up or would they go their separate ways and move on with their lives?

Needless to say, the assumption that all of last night had served to be a one night stand had arised upon Felicity's awakening. She looked around and curled up into a ball of subtle frustration as she frowned. Despite the rocky beginning she had been sure that the two had been hitting it off. At least... that's what she thought? Perhaps he had other intentions. Perhaps he was just like everyone else and was just looking for a quick roll in the hay before moving on to other things with much easier prey. And she had nearly been certain that she had been played.

"God *damnit!*"

"Good morning, princess."

Her eyes darted over to her doorway, where he had been standing with a cup of coffee and a bowl of cereal in hand. His hair was still messy from the night before as subtle traces of a sleepless night had painted a dopey yet smug smile on his face.

Asshole.

"You're still here?"

"Duh," he teased. "Did you not want me to be?"

She paused, pretending to have to think about it for a second. Of course she wanted him to be there. She really liked him and wanted to at least keep seeing him as a friend if nothing else.

"Oh Titania, how you wound me."

She snickered playfully, trying to chase away the negative thoughts ebbing away at her mind. "I don't raid a complete stranger's kitchen."

"I do when I know that I wore someone out."

"A little presumptuous, don't you think?"

"Should I try harder?"

She thought back to a similar conversation she had with someone nearly a lifetime ago. That person was no longer in the picture, yet she had brought him up in conversation. But it was time to move on. It was time to try and free herself from that bond and burn the bridge, despite the difficulty. "Do you want to?"

He nodded.

"I need you to tell me."

Dion moved to her side and sat on the bed, careful not to spill milk or coffee upon her mattress. "Do you?" he asked.

"Will you have me?"

His once sarcastic smile slowly turned into a flirtatious grin as he set her breakfast to the side. "If I do, will you try to be kinder to yourself as I am to you?"

She could feel him turn her to face him, sinking in well with his touch as he moved to tilt her chin up so that she was looking at him. He looked for any traces of doubt within the ocean of desire and hesitation.

"I will try," she finally responded.

THE HIDDEN ROOM
Susan Nordman

Welcome to Morpheus!"

The island was a paradise, just as Henry Young had told Maggie it would be. Located just off the western coast of Costa Rica, the lush, tropical jungles spilled down ancient volcanic spires into the Pacific Ocean. As the runabout glided over the edge of the reef, the water changed from deep ink to light turquoise. As she looked over the edge of the boat, Maggie was entranced by the colorful corals which seemed to dance in the clear waters. A dolphin riding their bow wave broke the mesmerizing spell of blue and yellow tangs darting through the waving anemones. Maggie had to laugh as the mammal chittered to her before returning to the deeper ocean.

"It's beautiful!" she shouted above the motor. "But wasn't Morpheus the god of sleep?"

"Originally, yes," Henry called back. "In Ovid's *Metamorphoses*, Morpheus was one of the sons of Somnus, the god of sleep, and appeared to people in their dreams as a human."

Of course, he knew; Henry knew everything. Her new husband could recite history like he had lived it and she hadn't asked a question yet he hadn't answered like an expert. As the scent of blossoming hibiscus and coconut filled the air, Maggie decided she'd test his knowledge of botany later, but not right now. The young bride was too content. They had planned to honeymoon on the island for two weeks so she'd have plenty of time to quiz him on the local plant life later.

As Maggie turned her head so the wind pushed her auburn hair out of her face, Henry slowed the boat to leave less of a wake for the sea creatures and so they didn't have to shout above the roar of the engine. "The official name of the island is Isla de los Sueños which translates to the Island of Dreams. My family bought it from the Costa Rican government several generations ago as a sanctuary for endangered species. There are several rare animals that live here and nowhere else."

"Why do you call it Morpheus?"

"No reason except that I liked the sound of it." Henry shrugged. "When I'm here, I can believe that any dream can come true."

"Aren't we going to dock?" Maggie asked when the boat continued to follow the shoreline around the island. Tantalizing floral aromas drifted to her on the gentle trade winds, but she didn't know what they were.

"Our house is on the west coast. The eastern portion of the island belongs to the Molonui."

"I thought you owned the whole island."

"On paper I do. The tribe is one of the endangered species I'm trying to protect. They're originally from Columbia, but moved to the island to avoid the conquistadors. They've lived here for generations and I don't need an entire island to myself. Besides that, the Molonui have nowhere else to go and still keep their traditions. Don't worry; they're good people and won't bother us."

Maggie wasn't sure about sharing the island with an

indigenous tribe, but she trusted her husband. If he said they were safe from the tribe, then she believed him.

Her husband! The thought that she and Henry were married made her lightheaded with happiness. Eight months ago, she didn't even know his name and now she was his wife and about to honeymoon on his—their—private island for two weeks.

The sun was cresting past its zenith when Henry entered the mouth of a perfectly round lagoon, a slightly deeper shade of blue than what was over the reefs, but still much lighter than the deeper ocean. Maggie couldn't see the house as he glided the boat up to the sturdy dock. Henry expertly jumped off and secured the boat to the cleat before offering Maggie his hand to help her down.

"Why didn't you build on the east side of the island?" Maggie asked as she lustfully eyed the protected sandy beach for an evening swim. "It would seem a little more protected from storms, but I don't know."

"That's actually a very good observation," Henry said, gesturing to the small cove with his free hand. "As a small island, there really isn't an area that doesn't get hit by Pacific storms and even hurricanes, but you are right that the most severe ones blow in on this side. The Molonui live on the east, so I was perfectly happy to build here. Besides, you can't see the sunsets from there and we get some great sunsets."

"Can I meet them sometime?"

"Who?"

"The Molonui."

"Absolutely," Henry said with a delighted smile. "We're good friends and I'm certain they'll want to meet you. I'll arrange it in the next few days, but it might not be as glamorous as you'd expect. Half of them wear their traditional clothes while the other half favor blue jeans. They're not ignorant of the outside world; they just want it to leave them alone."

"I can appreciate that." Maggie was about to ask

some more questions when they were interrupted by a middle-aged man and woman hurrying down the dock to greet them.

"Henry!" The woman smiled as she gave him a warm hug and kiss on the cheek. "We're so happy for you!"

After greeting them warmly, Henry's wide grin told Maggie he was very fond of the couple. "Maggie, I'd like to introduce Emma and Stu Palma, they take care of the place when I'm not here. Em, Stu, this is my wife Maggie."

As the man stepped in to give Henry a friendly handshake, the woman stepped towards Maggie. She hesitated, waiting to see how her open arms would be accepted by a stranger, and when Maggie returned her wide smile, she stepped forward and gave the younger woman a gentle hug of welcome.

"It's so good to meet you," Emma said, linking Maggie's arm in hers.

"Are you one of the Molonui?" Maggie asked shyly. She was bursting with curiosity about the other people on the island and wasn't sure how the question would be taken.

"No," she answered with an easy smile as if she'd expected it. "Stu is originally from Puerto Rico and I grew up in Florida. We were friends of Henry Senior until he died. When Henry took over the property, he kept our contract to maintain the residence and we've looked after both ever since. Don't tell Henry I told you this, but he's the spitting image of his father."

"I'm sorry I never got the chance to meet him," Maggie sighed. Actually, she wasn't all that sorry. As far as she knew, since Henry's mother had also passed, she didn't have any in-laws so she didn't have to worry about the drama of extended family members. She may regret it later, but she was inwardly relieved that she didn't have to worry about being rejected by them, either.

"It was long ago," Emma said with another warm smile, gently pulling Maggie's arm to guide her down the dock. "Now, you just come with me to the house and we'll just let the boys haul the bags up."

As the women walked away, Henry and Stu's voices followed them several paces down the dock before the words were blown away on the gentle trade winds.

"Is everything in place, Stu?" she heard Henry ask.

"Yes, sir," Stu answered. "When I received word that you had gotten remarried, I stocked the usual provisions."

"Thanks, Stu. What about…"

"So, when did you and Henry get married?" Emma asked, her question cutting off whatever Henry was about to ask. "I didn't even know he'd been seeing anyone, but then it's hard to receive messages way out here and he doesn't talk to us much."

"Uh, three days ago, but we've been dating for eight months," Maggie said, distracted by what she'd heard. "If I may, how did you know we were coming?"

"Carrier pigeon!" Emma said and then laughed when Maggie took her seriously. "Satellite phone, my dear. Henry calls us by satellite phone… or we call him if there's anything on el Sueño he needs to be aware of."

"Like what?"

"In our case, usually repairs to the house. Stu's great for minor fixes, but some storms require more labor and youth than what we can do and which the Molonui can graciously provide; in Henry's case, you. That was a surprise… a good surprise!"

The path turned and gently followed the hill giving Maggie the first glimpse of the house. Situated on the hill, she should have seen it when they entered the lagoon, but she and Henry had been talking and there was so much else for her to notice. Maggie imagined that in older times, the four-bedroom home would have been a mansion, but nestled against the tropical forest, it seemed more like a lavish bungalow and at once seemed both ancient and modern. Built in the plantation style of the south, columns supported a wrap-around porch on the upper level, but as time and tide had weathered the home, it had been updated and modernized. Being more of a "glamper" than a camper, Maggie couldn't help her inner relief as the solar panels glinting on the roof let her know she wouldn't be deprived of either cold drinks or hot showers.

Still arm in arm, the women entered the front door into a long hallway that looked as if it had been decorated a hundred years ago. To Maggie's uneducated eye, every lamp, table and chair looked to be a priceless antique.

The only item that didn't look as if it belonged in another era was a portrait of a young woman. While it wasn't indecent, it wasn't the usual art one found hanging in the foyer of a home. The model was wrapped in a blanket a bare shoulder and leg looked as if her nudity were about to be exposed. Her slight smile and dreamy eyes gave her the expression that she had just woken up from a blissful sleep and caught sight of her lover.

But something else was on her mind other than architecture and artwork. "Did I hear correctly that I'm not Henry's first wife?"

Emma frowned as dark clouds filled her light brown eyes. "Ah, I wasn't sure if you heard that, but no. Margaret, poor dear, died a few years ago. That's her portrait. I'm surprised Henry didn't tell you, but then again, maybe I'm not. He doesn't like to talk about her; it makes him sad."

"I can imagine," Maggie said staring at the portrait of the semi-nude woman. "May I ask how she died?"

"Boat accident, poor dear," Emma replied in an almost revenant whisper. "It happened just outside the lagoon. Henry said a bunch of kids ignored the protected status of the island and went scuba diving. I don't think they knew anyone lived here, but they weren't paying attention. Margaret was in a kayak; they didn't see her and ran their boat right over her. She drowned before Henry could get to her."

"That's awful! No wonder he hasn't spoken about it."

"Henry was shattered; this is the first time he's been back to los Sueños since it happened." Emma sighed, putting a comforting arm around Maggie's shoulders. "I suppose we should have taken the painting down, but Henry didn't tell us to and I'm afraid we didn't think of it with everything else we had to do to get ready for your arrival. It was a bit short notice for us, but we got it all done."

"She was lovely," Maggie admitted.

"Indeed, she was; inside and out. Henry painted it himself... oh, you didn't know he was an artist? Don't be at all surprised if he wants to paint you, too."

"In the nude?" Maggie couldn't help the bark of laughter. In her wildest dreams, she couldn't imagine posing like that. Even suggested nudity, was fine in a museum, but it wasn't for her. Well, not where other people could see it and the Palmas lived here when the Youngs weren't in residence.

"Only if you want to be captured that way," Emma said, but Maggie saw the corners of her mouth twitch at the young woman's prudishness.

Turning away from the portrait, Emma led her up the stairs to the second story. "Now, here's the master suite. The bathroom is through there. The mainland is such a long way away, I'm sure you want to rest and refresh yourself."

Suddenly exhausted and overwhelmed, Maggie decided a shower was exactly what she needed. As the hot water gently massaged her shoulders, she tried to let it rinse away her anxiety. She couldn't believe Henry hadn't told her he'd been married before. They'd known each other for nearly a year and, while she knew she couldn't possibly know everything about him in so short a time, she would have thought he'd at least have told her that.

While the shower didn't entirely relieve her anxiety, it did lessen the shock. Henry couldn't have been much older than Maggie was now. To have fallen in love and then lost her so abruptly, maybe she would also have been reluctant to talk about it in his situation. He would have given Margaret the same "until death do us part" vow at their wedding, oblivious to the tragedy that took her from him so soon.

Maggie couldn't help but smile at the thought as she reminded herself that "until death" had been her vows. Breaking the tradition of their traditional wedding, Henry promised to love Maggie for as long as he lived. One day, one of them would die leaving the other alone. A wave of love for her husband filled her that Henry had opened his heart to her in order to take that risk again.

Refreshed and more at ease with Henry's past, Maggie discovered when she stepped back into the bedroom, all of her clothes had been put away except a new beautiful, lacey sundress which had been laid out invitingly on the bed for her to try on. Her toiletries were also on the bed for her to put away now that she was finished in the shower.

Feeling like a schoolgirl, Maggie was delighted at the silky white fabric designed to catch the breeze and keep her cool in the tropical heat. It was as if the dress had been made specifically for her. After dressing, she couldn't contain her beaming smile as she joined Henry for dinner.

"Stu and Emma wanted to say goodbye, but they had to leave to make it back to the mainland before nightfall."

"I'm sorry I missed her," Maggie said, contrite that she wasn't even sure she'd thanked Emma for her kindness.

"Not to worry," Henry said, giving her a kiss on her cheek. "They'll be back next week with supplies. They live here when I'm away, but left to give us some privacy. We're on our honeymoon after all. Hungry?"

"Famished," Maggie admitted.

"I made crudités; being new to this climate, I wasn't sure if you'd want anything hot. I can fix you something else if you'd rather."

"No, cold food sounds much more appetizing right now. Thank you, sweetie."

Though Maggie considered crudités to be nothing more than an appetizer before the main meal, after a long day in the boat and getting settled, the light meal with a glass of chilled white wine was all she wanted. As usual, Henry was right and the meal sat very well on her stomach.

"Is there anything you can't do?" Maggie sighed happily. "Along with everything else, you're also a gourmet chef."

Giving her a shrug, Henry smiled. "I have the advantage of being wealthy. That in itself doesn't make me smart; what it gives me is time."

"What do you mean?"

"Time is something few people have enough of. Most people have enough money to get by and that gives them time enough to relax and spend with their families. While I work, I don't have a job I need to clock in to from nine to five every day and that gives me time to study everything I'm interested in. I'm an eternal student; when something new comes along that interests me, I go back to school."

"And where did you study the culinary arts?"

"Le Cordon Bleu in Paris."

"Where else?" Maggie smiled. "So, I assume you also speak French."

"Oui, Madam Young. Comme un indigéne."

"Showoff," Maggie scolded before looking away.

Henry frowned as he studied her expression. "What's bothering you? You've been quieter than usual this evening and I don't think it was the trip here."

Maggie sighed. She hadn't meant to give her misgivings away and had told herself it really wasn't that important and she did understand. "You didn't tell me you were married."

Henry's smile faltered as his eyes filled with pain. "No, I didn't. I apologize for not."

Offering Maggie his hand, Henry led her out into the hall to the beautiful portrait of Margaret. Standing behind his new wife, he wrapped his arm around her so they stood together under the image of his former spouse.

"Her name was Margaret…"

"I know; Emma told me. How long were you married?"

"She was killed in a boating accident three weeks before our fourth anniversary."

Maggie didn't know what to say so she said, "I'm sorry."

"So, was I," Henry said, kissing the back of her head. "Every day for years, missing her was all I thought about."

"What made you stop?"

"When I finally realized that by missing her, I was missing life. There comes a time when you the only thing left to do is pick up the pieces and get back to living. Please forgive me for not telling you. I never meant to hurt you; I just didn't know how to tell you."

"I know. I forgave you a couple of hours ago; I just wanted to hear you say it. But I need to know that you love me for me and that Maggie is not your way of replacing Margaret."

"Maggie," Henry said, turning her around so he could look deeply into her green eyes. "Never for one moment have I wished you were her. I knew I'd eventually fall in love again, but not for many more years. I couldn't believe it when you waltzed into my life. I won't lie to you, Mags; she was the love of my life. But Margaret is dead and you are not competing with a ghost. You are the love of my life now. Maggie, you amaze me."

"Well, I'll amaze you even more when you teach me to cook like you do," she told him, letting him know that the subject was officially closed. "I'd like to be able to surprise you with more than mac and cheese."

"Then lessons begin in the morning," Henry said, giving her a passionate kiss. Grabbing a new bottle of wine, he led her out to the veranda and together they watched the sunset. Maggie had to admit that he was right again. Sunrises were special; sunsets were spectacular.

Some time in the early morning, Maggie woke up to

scraping sounds and discovered Henry wasn't in bed with her. Deciding there must be an attic or crawl space in the rafters, she drifted back to sleep before her husband returned. The next morning, the portrait of Margaret was gone.

"I didn't mean for you to take her down," Maggie said dismayed. "She was a part of your life and I'm not jealous."

"I didn't think you were." Henry smiled. "But it was time. I'd like to put your portrait up instead."

Privately, Maggie made a note to tell Emma she'd been right that Henry would want to paint her.

But to her surprise, Henry didn't pull out his canvass and paints right away. Giddy again, the newlyweds spent the next few days back in honeymoon-mode thoroughly exploring the western portion of the island. Like a botanist who'd mastered his craft, Henry described in detail the various flowers of Morpheus while explaining how new life drifted on the wind and tides to populate remote volcanic islands. He stopped Maggie when she wanted to walk the perimeter of the los Sueños along the beaches. They weren't prepared for it and, even though the island was small, the jungle was dense enough for them to get into trouble if they weren't careful. He also hadn't been in touch with the Molonui and thought it would be rude to just barge in on them.

Trusting his instincts, Maggie contented herself with returning to their beach and baking herself in the sun; the ever-watchful Henry ushering her back inside before she could develop a nasty sunburn. Taking her hand, he led her into the parlor, now his painting studio complete with brushes, oils and an easel.

The last vestiges of jealousy over Margaret vanished when Henry didn't even suggest Maggie pose in the nude. Inwardly, she had expected him to want to recreate his late wife's portrait, but it seemed to not even occur to Henry. Instead, he insisted she'd look beautiful wearing the white sundress looking out in the west facing window to the sea, saying his goal as an artist was to capture her soul so he could remember it forever.

Being a model, Maggie learned, was hard work. Even if she had been laying down the way Margaret had been, it would have been difficult to control her impulses to move or even twitch. The portrait ended up taking a couple of days as standing without being able to move proved to be more exhausting than she expected. Fortunately, the light was constantly changing and Henry only had a short time each day for the conditions to be just right.

Though Maggie was dying to see the art, Henry wouldn't let her even peek at it until it was finished. Though it rankled her, she knew some artists could be rather finicky about things like that, so she respected Henry's wishes. But the more she thought about it, the more her insecurities returned. As she remembered her husband's comment about wanting to capture her soul in the paints, Maggie was suddenly overwhelmed with the desire to study Margaret's semi-nude image Henry had stored in the loft. In her mind, the picture had almost been alive; Margaret's eyes had burned with a fire that only the living seemed to possess, almost as if Henry had indeed captured her soul with his paints. Maggie's own portrait was a side profile. How could her soul compare to Margaret's full-on seductive stare?

If she were going to steal another look at Margaret, it had to be now. There was still another hour before the light would be right in the west facing window and Henry had gone down to the dock to check the motor on the boat.

Casually strolling out to the veranda, Maggie saw her husband walking down to the end of the pier. Perfect! She had just enough time to study the portrait before her husband came back. She felt a little guilty at sneaking behind his back, but she didn't want to upset Henry by asking about it. Maggie thought she'd just have her peek and her husband would be none the wiser.

Judging from the sounds she'd heard the other night, the loft had to have been just over her head in the master bedroom. On a hunch, Maggie looked inside the master closet where she found a set of stairs behind a real door rather than a pull-down ladder in the ceiling. The door wasn't hidden, but a relic feature from back when houses like this were common, but Maggie couldn't help feeling the electrical jolt of her discovery. An emergency flashlight hung from a hook by the stairs; Maggie took it and began to climb, feeling as if she'd found the portal into Narnia.

The attic was an antique collector's dream. Maggie thought the downstairs was magnificent enough with its French Renaissance chairs, Ming Dynasty vases and Colonial American cabinets, but stored away up here was furniture from every major period probably going back a thousand years. The items were priceless and Henry had them collecting dust in an attic.

What Maggie didn't find in the room was Margaret's portrait. Thinking she was just overlooking it among the other treasures, she decided to try again later when she noticed the hidden door. All but invisible against the far wall, what made the paneling stand out was half of a handprint etched in the dust like the corporeal evidence of ancient ghosts.

Gently pressing against the panel, Maggie heard a soft click; the door swung open to reveal a hidden room within the attic. The beam from her light highlighted the frames of dozens of paintings with Margaret's soul-filled eyes close to the door, watching Maggie as she entered. Feeling very much the intruder, Maggie saw a beautifully carved wooden box resting next to Margaret's portrait. Feeling a thousand eyes on her, she glanced apprehensively around the room before shining her flashlight into the box.

Maggie winced in surprise as something flashed and hit her eye in a prismatic brilliance. Catching her breath before looking again, Maggie saw the rainbow gleam had been from the light refracting through the facets of a huge diamond mounted in the center of an elaborate engagement ring. Along with the ring, the box contained matching wedding bands and several photographs of a very happy Henry and Margaret.

Maggie's heart sank as she flipped through the images. The last item was Margaret's obituary.

Margaret Owens Young sadly passed away on July 14, 2011 at the age of 24 after a boating accident off the coast of Costa Rica where she had been celebrating her fourth anniversary with her husband of four years, Dr. Henry Young.

Funeral services will be held on Saturday, July 23rd at St. Mark's in San Antonio. In lieu of flowers, the family requests donations be made to charities for leukemia research, a passion for Henry and Margaret after they lost Margaret's brother to the disease.

Margaret is survived in death by her husband Henry, parents Will and Jane Owens and sister Elaine.

The clipping continued to describe Margaret's passion for adventure, her love of horses and cosplaying at sci-fi conventions. Sure enough, Maggie saw one of the pictures was of Margaret complete with Vulcan ears and Henry almost unrecognizable in superb Klingon garb.

Maggie couldn't help smile in relief as she fully accepted the fact that she wasn't the rebound wife; she and Margaret were as polar opposites as two people could get. If Henry had been trying to recreate his love for her, there were hundreds of other women who wouldn't think twice about posing in the nude or walking down the streets in a Star Trek uniform.

Even so, Maggie couldn't help the wave of melancholy flood her heart as she realized how much they had been in love. And all Henry had left to show for it fit in this small box.

Her guilt returned as she realized she'd snooped long enough; this part of Henry's life was off limits until he was ready to discuss it. Gently closing the box, Maggie placed back where she had found it. But as she swung the light around to make sure she wouldn't trip over anything on her way out the door, the beam illuminated another portrait of another beautiful young woman; her captivating eyes held onto Maggie's and wouldn't let go.

Like Maggie's own portrait downstairs, this woman was fully clothed, but that was where the difference ended. Instead of a sundress staring pensively out to sea, this girl was in faded blue jeans torn at the knees which were spread as she held a beer between them; her bare feet were planted firmly on a low coffee table, which Maggie recognized as the one in the living room. Though the woman's head was tossed back in laughter, her brilliant eyes still managed to look into Maggie's.

Beside this portrait was another box also filled with photos and wedding rings. According to her obituary, Stella Dante had died in a car crash at the age of thirty-two.

Maggie began to hyperventilate; the room was filled with paintings, each with a box of yellowing paper commemorating her life and recording her death: Wendy Martin, died of cancer; Mary Wright, natural causes; Grace DiMarco; car crash.

Every obituary held the same words: *survived by her husband Henry Young!*

Oh, god! There were dozens of them, trophies preserved in this dark, windowless mausoleum. These weren't portraits, they were death masks! How long did she have before her own portrait joined them? How soon until her own untimely accident?

Panic gripped Maggie when it occurred to her that she'd lost track of time. Henry would be back from the boat any minute! If he knew she'd found his trophy room, she either wouldn't last the night or would have an "unfortunate accident" in the next few days. He'd planned a hiking trip to the east of the island to meet the Molonui; how easy it would be for her to lose her footing on the sharp, volcanic soil.

Maggie sensed the longer she could keep from Henry that she knew his secret, the longer she would live. Margaret had been married to him for almost four years until she had been killed. Maggie held no doubts she'd discovered his hidden room before her boating accident. Margaret's obituary said Henry was a doctor. Though she had been killed in an apparent accident, Mary had died of natural causes. It began to dawn on the terrified Maggie that he could kill her half a dozen ways and not leave evidence that would be looked for in an autopsy.

Glancing around the room to make sure everything was back the way she'd found it, Maggie raced to the door only to turn back at the threshold as self-preservation warred with her sense of duty. Maggie didn't want to die especially at the hands of the man who had promised to love her... until death. But how could she abandon these women? Hers was the only living voice who could attest to their true fate.

The only way off the island was by boat. Though Maggie had never driven one before in her life, she was certain she could aim it towards the mainland once she got it out of the lagoon. Immediately, she rejected the idea as Henry might be down there this very minute rigging her own little "accident".

Another option was waiting for the Palmas to return. If Emma and Stu arrived on schedule, they'd be back on Los Sueños day after tomorrow with supplies. Maggie could leave with them assuming she survived that long.

And assuming they weren't in on it! Paranoia dashed Maggie's hopes that they might help her. They had known about Margaret and had lived in this house for years when Henry wasn't in residence. Did her super-wealthy husband pay them exorbitant amounts of money to look the other way? Maggie had to assume they knew; from this moment on, she could only rely on herself.

The Molonui might help, but it was unlikely. She'd never met them and didn't even know if they spoke English. Besides that, they were friends with Henry. For all she knew, they kept his secret so they could live unhindered on his island.

What else could she do? Emma had mentioned a

satellite phone which was probably in Henry's study downstairs. Once he was asleep, she could look for it; she'd found his hidden room so she'd find the phone. Once she called for help, she'd have to wait until help arrived. Her very survival depended on Henry being oblivious to the fact that Maggie knew his secret.

Maggie once more froze in the door, unable to leave these poor women even as she desperately tried to avoid their fate. If she left now without any evidence, it would be impossible to convince the authorities to what she had seen. Henry was freakishly smart. If he suspected she'd seen his hidden room, Maggie was certain every scrap of evidence proving Henry's crimes would vanish.

Surviving without the evidence to stop him from moving on to his next bride would only delay the inevitable. Without anything corroborating her story, she'd still die. It would just a slower death as guilt corroded her soul.

No, Maggie said to herself, she couldn't, *wouldn't* leave. She owed it to all of those women discarded in his secret room to at least try. Henry had been careless by leaving Margaret's portrait hanging on the wall. That one mistake might be the only one he'd ever made or will ever make. As the latest in a long line of victims who knew his secret, Maggie had to make sure she would be the last.

Cell service was unavailable on the island, but Maggie had kept her phone charged in order to use the camera. As quickly as she could, she pulled it out and began snapping pictures of the paintings along with the evidence from the boxes intending to send them in an email to her father along with a message explaining what had happened. If she died, he wouldn't get the message until her phone pinged a tower back on the mainland, but at least he'd know what Henry really was.

Not all of the boxes had photos; the more she opened, the further back in time she seemed to go until the sepia images almost faded out entirely. Many more boxes didn't have camera images, but sketches signed with Henry's flourishing signature on aging yellow paper.

But it was the obituaries Maggie wanted the most. The paintings, while detailing his former wives, just might be the work of a prolific artist, the obits would be documented in newspaper archives. That evidence alone of Henry surviving so many wives would be suspicious enough to warrant an investigation.

As another insurance policy, Maggie took the sketches, newspaper clippings and rings from four of the women, intending to hide them in her suitcase. If he didn't know they were there, Henry might not find them before someone else did.

Satisfied she'd done everything she could, Maggie turned to leave only to see Henry blocking the door.

"There is a light, if you want," Henry said flipping the switch so the glare from the harsh bulb highlighted his muscular frame.

"I know everything," Maggie blurted, her grip tightening on the flashlight handle. Whatever happened, she was not going to go down without a fight. She'd most likely lose against someone of Henry's size and build, but one good crack to his skull would leave a mark he couldn't explain away when her family came looking for her.

For some reason, her comment seemed to amuse him. Maggie flushed with anger as a slight smile pulled the edges of his mouth. She may be at his mercy, but how dare he mock her!

"I know *everything*," she repeated belligerently, almost daring him to contradict her.

"I doubt that," his eye twinkling at some private joke. "Not even Stu and Emma know the truth and they know me better than anyone."

Maggie's sudden rush of adrenaline was almost painful as surging hope suddenly ignited every nerve in her body. The Palmas didn't know! She just had to make sure she stayed alive until they got here.

The smile faded from Henry's face as he read his wife's unmistakable expression. "They'll be here day after tomorrow in the early morning," he almost whispered, his shoulders deflating like a slow leak from a helium balloon. "I'll arrange for them to take you to the mainland if you like."

It had to be a trick for Maggie to lower her guard. She didn't fall for it and gripped the flashlight more tightly. When he took a step towards her, she raised it in warning for him to keep his distance. Though she'd never harmed a living thing in her life, in that instant, Maggie knew she had it within herself to aim true if he got too close.

To her utter surprise, Henry stepped well around her before sitting cross-legged a few feet away, just far enough that he wasn't immediately threatening. Maggie didn't know if it was deliberate or not, but she was fully aware that when he seated himself, Henry was no longer blocking the door. She'd be down the stairs before he could stand again and there were knives in the kitchen!

With his hands resting dejectedly on his knees, Henry gave no intention of becoming the violent killer she believed she'd married. "I'll tell you the truth, if you want to hear it. but I doubt it'll be any more believable than what you already think of me."

"Okay." Maggie was wary; torn between wanting to hear what he had to say that could possibly explain all this away and letting her chance for escape slip away. He looked wounded, but Maggie wasn't fooled. Injured animals were always the most dangerous.

"And I am sorry I didn't tell you sooner, but I never know how someone is going to react."

"How did you think I was going to react to... to *this*?"

"Considering that you think I killed all these women; I would expect you're terrified. Please, don't be. I didn't kill them and I have no intention of murdering you. Maggie, the unbelievable truth is that I'm immortal."

"Right!" she scoffed, her eyes narrowing in disbelief. It probably wasn't a wise idea to mock a deranged psychopath, but she couldn't help it. "What are you... some kind of vampire?"

Henry actually laughed. "Hardly. As I'm sure you've noticed, I don't turn to ash in the sunlight nor do I exist on a diet of blood."

"If you're not a vampire, then what are you?"

"Good question," he said running his fingers through is hair as if he were trying to decide on an answer. "Human, I think... at least I still consider myself human. The only difference between us is that my cells continually regenerate. I haven't aged in over eight hundred years."

When her eyes narrowed again, Henry continued, "I'm afraid it's true. I was born in 1192 in England during the reign of King John... you remember, the Magna Carta King John? It wasn't the greatest time to be alive and it was even worse being a serf. Without the possibility of land or title, when I was sixteen, I became a sailor. After many adventures which I won't bore you with, our ship went down in a storm. Myself and five other shipmates got to a life boat and were the first Europeans to discover the South America. Of course, we had no idea where we were at the time and were just grateful to be alive."

"I'm not an idiot," Maggie snapped. "I do know some history and Balboa discovered South America in 1513."

"Officially, yes," Henry said, unperturbed that she was trying to poke holes in his tale. "Even I'll admit that as long as we'd already been sailing the seas, it's possible my crewmates and I weren't the first, either. The Vikings had been in North America for centuries, so who's to say other Europeans hadn't been washed ashore also? The difference is that Balboa returned to tell others of his discovery. Contrary to Columbus, most of us did know the world was round; it was just a lot larger than we expected. Up until this point, we didn't know there were other continents."

"So, what stopped you from entering the history books?"

"For us, there was no one to tell. We were stranded and our little lifeboat barely got us there in the first place; it wasn't going to get us back. While I can't be sure, I think we landed somewhere around what is now Caracas, Venezuela. We began exploring and discovered several indigenous tribes, one of them being the Molonui."

"The people on the other side of this island."

"Yes, and I'll get to that later. For now, all I knew was that they were a kind people and took us in."

While he said this, Henry reached for a box. Most of the boxes were elaborately carved, but this particular one was without adornments. The only markings Maggie could see were the gentle scratches of wear marring its ancient surface. Carefully opening it so he wouldn't appear threatening, Henry and took out a pencil sketch so detailed, it could have been a photograph. He gazed longingly at it for a moment before handing it to Maggie with a sigh. "That was Itcha, my first wife."

"She's beautiful," Maggie said bitterly, noting her elegant grace and long wavy hair framing a delicately oval face. The dark eyes staring back at her expressed both a strength and vulnerability that Maggie was sure many men would be drawn to. As she examined it, she noticed the delicate portrait was on vellum.

"Yes, she was. I was twenty-four at the time I met the Molonui and I became friends with their chief, Tauma. I also fell in love with his daughter, Itcha, but I made no advances towards her. I had no plans to stay and wasn't going to ask her to leave her people."

"So, what happened?" Maggie asked curious to know where his story was going. Did he really believe she was stupid enough to believe he couldn't die?

Henry continued, "We lived with them for several weeks, but when it was time to leave, the men I was with became violent. The one thing the Molonui had in abundance was what we Europeans lusted after: gold. If they had asked, the tribe would have let them take enough to live a wealthy life if they could ever get it back to England, but they didn't ask and they didn't stop with the gold. I was just as enraged as Tauma when they began raping the women. To the Molonui's surprise, I fought with them against my own people."

Looking Maggie in the eye, Henry said, "This wasn't murder; I've never *murdered* anyone."

Henry was silent for a moment when Maggie only nodded. Studying her cautious expression, he could see that, while she was still reserving judgement on his fantastic story, she did accept the difference.

"To thank me, Tauma gave Itcha to me as a wife and they held a ceremony making me a member of the tribe. Part of the ceremony had me drink a special tea and they declared I was the tribe's protector for as long as the tribe drew breath. I knew it was a great honor they were giving me, but not being born into the tribe, I didn't know the full extent of that honor."

"Immortality," Maggie said skeptically.

"Yes, of course, I didn't know it then. As years passed, Itcha and I never had any children of our own, so we cared for the orphans of the village, kids who'd lost their parents to sickness or accidents. We were very happy for about ten years until she became sick and died."

"I'm sorry," Maggie said, though she wasn't really.

"Yeah, me, too. I was devastated. I loved my adopted people and continued to live with them for another ten years."

Maggie narrowed her eyes again as his story stopped making sense. "That's impossible. You'd have been like forty-four by this time."

"Immortal," Henry reminded her. "And I was actually forty-eight. It was only now that I was beginning to understand the full impact of the ceremony that made me protector of the village. It wasn't for as long as I drew breath, but as long as the *tribe* did. It was a cultural misunderstanding; Tauma thought I knew. I didn't, but it was done. The potion they gave me made me immortal. Maggie, all this happened in the twelfth century. I know it's hard to believe, but I'm over eight hundred years old. And I didn't kill these women; I just outlived them."

"Did they know about you?" she asked, trying to keep him talking.

"Most of them, yes. Some I told before we married which didn't always go well. Considering we were in the Middle Ages, a few of them thought is was dark magic or a curse of the devil and wanted nothing to do with me once they knew. Others were able to accepted it. Some, like Amelia there, hated watching herself age while I stayed young and left me later in life. But I still loved her, just as I love you. And this is my curse: to outlive everyone I love."

"Then why do you do it?"

"I may be immortal, but I'm also still human. I admit, it was exciting at first. Eternal life; it's the dream of people the world over and I had it. It was when my second wife died that I began to fully grasp my fate. Umah was also a Molonui and for a time, we were also very happy. She died in my arms at the age of eighty-one. I was a hundred and twenty-nine and I still looked like I was in my late twenties.

"Following Umah's death, I became bitter and left the tribe, but my curse followed me. If I had a normal lifespan, I would have either died before I had a chance to fall in love again or died in my bitterness. Understanding that life, love and even pain ebbs and flows has been one of the advantages. As we continue to live, we heal and eventually, we are open to fall in love again."

Maggie couldn't help the sting pricking her heart. "So, I'm just the next woman in line so you aren't lonely."

Henry was shocked, "God, no, Maggie. I've actually lived most of my life alone, but when the chance comes that I do fall in love, I hold on to it with everything I have. Maybe I should have told you before, but I was just so happy to have found you so soon after Margaret. I was selfish; I didn't want it to end. It has, you know. Not everyone can accept what I am."

"Is there a way to break the curse?"

With a smile, Henry considered it. "I think so, but it's unthinkable. In the ceremony, I was made protector for as long as there were Molonui. Since the potion worked and I'm still alive, I can only assume that when the last Molonui dies, so will I. The tribe may only live on this one island, but they live. To end my immortality would mean genocide."

"That would be unthinkable," Maggie agreed, wishing he didn't sound so confident. Just one waver in his voice would convince her that not even he believed his outlandish tale. An idea hit her and she tried another tactic. "Could you make someone else immortal?"

Now it was Henry's turn to warily narrow his eyes at her implied suggestion. "The Molonui probably could, but even for you I wouldn't ask them. The greatest part of being immortal is finding someone like you to share my life with. But you called it a curse and it is. When I fell in love with you, it was knowing full well that one day I will have to sacrifice that happiness because one day, through death or desertion, you *will* leave me."

"But if you could make me immortal, I wouldn't have to."

"No, Maggie." Henry shook his head vigorously. "Not even for you. In this digital age where the entire world is photographed and documented constantly, it's hard enough for me to keep myself hidden. With two immortals always on the run, it would be almost impossible. But even if you were willing to do such a thing, I wouldn't allow it. Discovery is a very real threat. It was easier a couple of centuries ago when people believed I was immortal through magic or an act of god. If today's people knew that a potion made me what I am,

I'd be dissected so scientists could learn how it was done and then recreate it for the masses. That thought gives me the chills. It wouldn't be the Mother Teresa's of the world continuing their good works throughout the ages, but the Kim Jong Uns, Vladimir Putins and the Donald Trumps. Never!"

Maggie stared at Henry in shock. She had never seen such passionate anger in him before.

"You still don't believe any of this," Henry said. Though his head was bowed, he was looking up at her. Then he suddenly smiled. "You're testing me. Very well, ask anything you want."

"How can I believe it? Everything in this room could have been fabricated to fit your story. The paintings, all of which you created; the obituaries could have been forged."

Henry nodded. "And the photographs could all have been doctored. The only solid evidence I can give you is time. Give me enough time and you will one day believe."

"How many women are in this room?" Maggie heard herself asking. "How many wives have you had?"

"Including you, I've loved forty-two women, but I've only been married thirty-one times. A few discovered the truth before we wed and didn't go through with it. But I loved them anyway. In the end, we're all human."

"Did you kill them?"

"Only one," Henry admitted.

"You *are* a murderer!" Maggie hunched down, ready to strike, but he didn't move from the floor.

"It depends on how you view a mercy," he said evenly, never breaking his steady gaze. "Denise, that's her there, had a brain tumor. At least, that's what I believe she was dying from. It was long before x-rays and MRIs could diagnose such things. She was in agony so I deliberately overdosed her in order to ease her suffering. Yes, it was murder, but I didn't get a psychopathic thrill from it."

"Have you ever killed anyone else?"

"Only as a soldier in war. I don't fight often as my

immortality gives me an unfair advantage, but yes, I have fought and killed when I believed in the cause. I wasn't in America during the Revolutionary War, but I fought with the North during the Civil War. I joined the Allies during both of the World Wars and I refused service during Viet Nam."

"Any others?"

"Plenty, but I mention those because I have history books on my shelves downstairs with my photograph. Granted, these pictures could also have been doctored or it was my many-times great grandfather, but that is for you to decide. Next question."

Maggie wasn't sure if she wanted to know, but the words tumbled out before she could call them back. "I'm just twenty; if you're so old, what did you see in me?"

Henry paused before answering, giving her another amused smile. "Answer me this first: if you thought I had killed these women, why did you stay in this house? Why didn't you get out when you had the chance?"

"Because I needed evidence; even if I died, I had to make sure you couldn't do this to anyone else."

Without seeming to move a muscle, as if by magic, his smile tenderly transformed into the one Maggie had fallen in love with. "And that is exactly why I love you. You would sacrifice your own life to protect women you don't even know. Maggie, I don't think you realize how extraordinarily exceptional you are. Do you still believe I killed these women?"

Maggie hesitated, still unsure.

"Okay," Henry said, "then answer me this: do you believe I'm going to kill you?"

"No," she answered, but it wasn't until she actually said the words that Maggie trusted she was safe. It wasn't Henry's story, his unbelievable tale of magic potions and extremely long life that convinced her, but the one thing he hadn't done that helped heal her shattered confidence. In all the time he told his tale, he hadn't tried to even touch her.

With his strength, she would have been disarmed in seconds if that had been his goal, but he never once even tried to rise from the floor.

"I'm glad," Henry said, his melancholic voice filled with relief. "I'm going to go downstairs now. Stay up here if you like, look at everything you want to. This was the only secret I kept from you. If there's anything else you want to know, just ask. I hope you'll stay with me, but Stu and Emma will be here soon if you still want to leave."

Unable to speak, Maggie watched him walk slowly to the door before pausing. "Maggie, do you remember our vows to each other?"

"Of course, I do: To love one another until death do us part."

"No." Henry looked back at her, his sad eyes full of hope in his last bid to convince her. "Those were your vows. I promised to love you for the rest of my life. In over eight hundred years, I have never broken that promise and I never will."

Late in the afternoon the next day, Henry stood on the western veranda, momentarily losing sight of the boat in the glare of the setting sun before Stu turned to follow the island coast back to the east. They should just make it there before it was fully dark. On the other side of the island, he could faintly hear the drums of the Molonui.

In the mid-16th Century when it had become clear to Henry his tribe would never be safe from the old world determined to exploit the new, he began taking steps to ensure their survival. After years of searching, he found Isla de los Sueños and moved the entire village to its isolated shores. Centuries later, when the Molonui were threatened again by modern explorers and developers, he fought governments in order to have the island established as an environmental sanctuary for the rare seabirds and turtles that migrated to its shore. So far, it had worked; the developers were forced to stay away and the endangered species he so loved still thrived.

But Henry knew it wouldn't last. After eight hundred and thirty-six years, the one thing he'd learned with an absolute certainty was that everything died and that would include himself one day when the Molonui were gone forever. It was inevitable. With all his wealth and power, not even Henry could stay their execution forever. The oceans were rising, the climate was warming and his people were dying. Henry estimated that within the next century, there wouldn't be anyone left for him to protect and when that day came Henry the Younger of Kent, England would die.

But until that day came, Henry Young would give everything he had for those he loved.

As he watched the Palmas vanish around the reef, Henry felt Maggie's warm hands wrap around his waist. With a smile, she rested her head against her husband's chest while they watched the undulating wake scatter the pillar cast from the setting sun into thousands of fires dancing across the lagoon.

Gently, as if he were afraid a sudden movement would wake him from his happiness, Henry placed his arm around her shoulders. Once he had witnessed the look of terror in her eyes after she'd found his shrine to his former loves, he had been certain he'd lost Maggie forever. He could scarcely believe it when she came to him later, reaffirming her love for him and her intention to stay. When he asked what had convinced her, all she would answer was *time*.

Time at least was the one thing Henry could give her in abundance. Not even an immortal could know how much of it they would have together, but whatever they did have, they would both love each other for the rest of their lives.

Maggie knew Henry believed that he'd convince her in time, but the truth was she already believed and the evidence that had finally convinced her had been in the hidden room. After he had left her, Maggie had gone through every box and found the proof she needed to lay aside her doubts and believe.

Not all of the smiling, happy women had been captured in the flowering of their youth. Some were middle-aged while others had been elderly; many of the boxes held drawings of the same woman progressing from youth into her golden years. And all of the images had been carefully drawn by the same, loving hand on paper that aged and withered the farther back in time she traveled until the brittle, yellow leaves were almost too fragile to hold.

Looking around the hidden room, Maggie believed; not in the sepia photographs that were so faded the images were barely there at all nor in the masterfully crafted portraits that had darkened over the centuries. She believed in the promise her husband had given her on their wedding day: to love her for the rest of his life.

Maggie had found that love... in time.

THE COURTSHIP
David Martyn

The sun was high in the morning sky when Rachel shook the man in the bed. "Get up! You promised you would find work. The day is half gone. Get up!"

The man groaned, "Leave me woman. Let me sleep. If the day is half gone, there is always tomorrow."

"Wash your face while I make you breakfast."

The man sat up in the bed. His eyes still closed, he took a deep breath, stretched his neck and then his back. He straightened his arms and drew his shoulders back and yawned. He opened his eyes and sighed. He smiled when Rachel walked by, grabbed her and pulled her onto the bed. Holding her close, he kissed her.

"Come to bed. First pleasure, then breakfast."

Rachel pulled herself away. "You want to please me, find work and marry me."

"I work."

"You steal. Find honest work and let me be an honest wife."

"Marry you? You—an honest wife?" The man began

to laugh.

"An honest wife? You joke! How many husbands have you had? Too many for me to count! No husband will make you an honest woman. You will never be accepted by the women of Sychar. Get used to it, Rachel, your whole life has been one man's bed after another. You take our money in trade for giving us moments of pleasure. A leper would be more welcome with the women of this town than you will ever be!"

"Get out! Get out and don't come back!"

The man did not look up. He sat at the table leaning over his meal with an arm wrapped around the plate in front of him. "I'm leaving—after I eat. Then you can sneak about in the hot sun out of the eyes of the neighbors. I will be back for supper."

Rachel walked to the window. "Eat your breakfast and be gone!"

She could see the women returning from the well and said to herself, "I want to go as soon as they are all back, before the sun gets any hotter."

On a dusty road outside of the village of Sychar, a Jewish rabbi and his disciples slowly made their way north from Jerusalem. For most, it was their first journey through Samaria. Good Jews did not travel through Samaria. These men of Galilee would instead add days to their journey to and from the Temple to avoid any contact with this unclean half-breed people.

When Jesus first saw the walls of Sychar on the horizon, he asked Peter, "Simon Peter, tell me the story of your courtship. How did you meet your wife?"

Simon looked up from the dusty path, smiled and said, "I first saw her at the well in Bethsaida. She would go in the morning with the women and maidens. She was beautiful—and such a smile! I knew at once I must charm her and then seek her father's permission."

Jesus smiled. "Charm her? How?"

Peter was nodding his head and smiling brightly, "Well, Master, I was most subtle of course. I would bow deeply as she passed and say, 'tidings to the beauty of Bethsaida.'"

Jesus laughed. "Yes, I see. Very subtle."

Peter continued, "She smiled back! One day she said, 'A handsome, prosperous and wise man would bring a basket of fresh fish and meet my father.'"

"And when did you do so?"

Peter laughed. "That very day. She is a most amazing woman."

Jesus still smiling replied, "She caught her fish—a woman who knows her heart and acts." After a pause, Jesus added, "You love her very dearly. Yet you are here with me."

"Truly rabbi, I do love her. But she knows I love you, as does she. She cannot journey with you, but I can. She is always with me as I walk with you."

"She is a great help to Mary and the others."

Jesus stopped and looked at the village ahead, then up at the bright sun in the cloudless sky above. Turning he looked into Peter's eyes and said, "The Father above has given you a great love. The well—it is a good sign. Jacob met his love Rachel at the well in Haran. It was the same well where Abraham's servant found Rebekah. He prayed for a sign of God's chosen one—the sign that a woman would give him water and his camels as well. Rebekah was dearly loved by Isaac. She was chosen just as Isaac was chosen. And Moses too—Moses met his wife, Zipporah at the well. You see then, my friend, you are in good company."

Peter smiled and walked on silently. As they made their way toward Sychar, Peter spoke up. "We must stay on the road around the town, I dread the thought of encountering Samaritans. It is good that we pass by in the heat of the sun. Few will be about."

"We have encountered Arameans, Greeks, even

Romans. Do you fear Samaritans?"

"Rabbi, they have disobeyed God's law. They have married people of the outside. They do not worship at the Temple in Jerusalem but in their idolatrous temple on Mount Gerizim! The Romans never knew our law or the One True God. But they—rabbi, do not forget how Samaritans desecrated the Holy Temple with the bones of men—the Samaritans have offended and abandoned God!"

"Peter, do you hate the Samaritans?"

Peter's eyebrows tightened as he collected his thoughts. "It is written, 'love what is good, hate what is evil.'"

Jesus looked towards Sychar and asked, "What prophet has not called for God's people to repent with warnings of His wrath to come? What prophet was not stoned, thrown down a well, cut in two or murdered? How many times has our Heavenly Father delayed His judgment, waiting that some might repent?"

Peter's face cringed at the words. "But our people were sent into slavery, in Egypt and later Babylon."

"And how did they repay God's salvation from Egypt, the land where they grew in number, with labor, yes but also homes, food and safety? Their faith was weak. They complained to Moses. They doubted their God who led them, and they wandered the desert for forty years."

Jesus turned to Peter and smiled. "Even in His wrath He loved them. Does any father find joy in the misery that rebellion and sin bring to his children? It is the misery of sin that He abhors, and it is the gift of His love that He sends. Should even a Samaritan be punished for the sins of his father? No, let each man or woman be accountable for their own sin. And let each man or woman find the salvation sent to them by their Father in heaven who loves them."

Jesus shook the dust from his head scarf, stomped the dirt from his hot sandaled feet and resumed walking the road. Master and disciples followed the path as it wound its way around the city where they came to a crossroad. To the left the road led into the heart of Samaria. Ahead lay the way to Galilee. To the right was the road to the city gate. A tree was planted by the crossing and near the tree was an ancient well. Jesus walked to the tree, leaned his walking stick against it and sat down, shaded from the blazing sun. The air was still and hung heavy in the heat of the day.

"Judas," he called out.

A lanky man wearing the best robe in the group came over. "Yes, rabbi?"

"Judas, you carry the money, go into the village and buy food. We shall not stop in another city before Galilee. Take your time and find bread, figs, raisins and dried fish. Buy wine, and water and wine skins, for each of us."

"That is much to carry, master."

"All of you are to go. I will wait here."

Turning to Peter, James, and John he said, "Do not fear the Samaritans. Do not call their food unclean. It is not what goes into the mouth that defiles you; you are defiled by the words that come out of your mouth."

Jesus leaned back against the tree and closed his eyes. "Go."

As the disciples trudged off towards the foreboding city of the despised Samaritans, they could overhear Jesus begin his prayer. "Father, send her out to me…"

Rachel scanned the street from her window. It was empty. She glanced at the man at the table, bent over his still warm cakes and figs. She opened the door and stepped out. Seeing the disciples walking towards her she thought, *Who are they? Jews? In Sychar?* She stepped back inside her door. The man at the table did not look up. "I thought you were going to the well. There better be water when I return."

"I'm going. There is a large group of Jews coming in—to the market I suppose. I will wait until they pass. Why would Jews come here?"

"Who knows? A large group? Are they armed?"

"I did not see swords. They are not soldiers."

"For all their sanctimony, Jews are cowards. Perhaps one has come to collect a debt and needs a mob to protect him!"

"They have passed—walking towards the market. I am going."

Rachel stepped out the door, picked up her large water jug, placed it on her shoulder and walked towards the city gate. The narrow streets provided shade, but outside the gate the heat of the sun quickly made its presence felt. Even though empty, the water jar dug into her shoulder and sweat began to run from her brow. *At least there is some shade at the well,* she thought. *Will I ever again be able to draw my water in the cool of day?*

Rachel stopped at the well and set down her jug. She took the rope tethered to a stake beside the well and tied it the jug. She began to lower the jug, careful not to break it against the stone sides of the well. Hand over hand, she lowered the jug waiting to hear the soft splash as it found the water.

"Give me a drink."

The words startled Rachel. She turned and saw a man sitting beneath the shade tree. Another Jew.

"How is it you, a Jew, ask for a drink from me, a woman of Samaria?"

Jesus stood up and brushed the dust from his robe. He smiled and said, "If you knew the gift of God and who it is that is saying to you, 'Give me a drink,' you would have asked him and he would have given you living water."

Rachel stared at Jesus a few moments and replied, "Sir, you have nothing to draw water with, and the well is deep. Where do you get that living water?"

Rachel paused and watched Jesus. He smiled back at her. His smile captivated her. She needed to turn away before—

She turned to the well. "Are you greater than our

father, Jacob? He gave us the well and drank from it himself, as did his sons and his livestock."

Still smiling, Jesus said, "Everyone who drinks of this water will be thirsty again. But whoever drinks of the water that I will give him will never be thirsty again. The water that I will give him will become in him a spring of water welling up to eternal life."

His words drew her gaze back to him. "Sir, give me this water, so that I will not be thirsty or have to come here to draw water."

Jesus nodded. His smile gone, he said, "Go call your husband and come here."

Rachel immediately replied, "I have no husband."

Jesus' eyes burned into hers. "You are right in saying, 'I have no husband;' for you have had five husbands, and the one you now have is not your husband. What you have said is true."

Rachel's jaw dropped, but her eyes remained focused on the eyes of Jesus. "Sir, I perceive you are a prophet."

Rachel had to close her eyes and break the stare of Jesus. Then opening them again and looking away she said, "Our fathers worshipped on this mountain, but you say that in Jerusalem is the place where people ought to worship."

His words brought her eyes back to him, "Woman, believe me, the hour is coming when neither on this mountain nor in Jerusalem will you worship the Father. You worship what you do not know; we worship what we know, for salvation is from the Jews."

Jesus paused, and seeing she was listening closely continued, "But the hour is coming, and is now here, when the true worshippers will worship the Father in spirit and in truth, for the Father is seeking such people to worship him. God is spirit and those who worship him must worship in spirit and truth."

Rachel replied, "I know that the Messiah is coming, he who is called Christ. When he comes, he will tell us all things."

Again, Jesus' eyes stared into her soul. "I who speak to you am he."

Both stood silently, their eyes locked together.

The moment was interrupted by the sound of the disciples plodding footsteps as they returned from Sychar. Slowly they encircled Jesus and Rachel. Each of them wondered what was happening. But none, not even Peter could ask 'Why are you talking with her?' They stood there in the hot sun watching Jesus as their dust settled around them.

Rachel turned and walked away, back to Sychar, leaving her water jug behind.

As she made her way to the city gate, her pace quickened. At the gate she began to run. She ran to the market shouting, "Come see a man who told me everything I ever did! Can this be the Christ?"

Once Rachel left, the disciples followed Peter into the shade. "Let's eat," he said, and he opened one of the baskets.

Jesus stood at the well watching Rachel. Peter called out, "Rabbi eat!"

Not turning from his gaze, he replied, "I have food to eat that you do not know about."

One of them asked, "Has anyone brought him something to eat?"

Jesus turned around and walked over to them under the shade. "My food is to do the will of him who sent me and to accomplish his work. They say, 'There are yet four months and then comes the harvest.' Look, I tell you, lift up your eyes, and see that the fields are white for harvest."

Instinctively, the disciples looked out at the valley below, Jesus continued, "Already the one who reaps is receiving wages and gathering fruit for eternal life, so that sower and reaper may rejoice together. For here the saying holds true, 'One sows, and another reaps.' I sent you to reap that for which you did not labor."

The disciples looked at each other in silence, as Jesus

said, "Others have labored that you may enter their labor."

Jesus sat down, leaned against the tree and closed his eyes. One by one the disciples began to eat—in silence.

In the market of Sychar, Rachel boldly and urgently recounted her encounter with the Jewish prophet at the well. "He told me all I ever did! I tell you he is a prophet! He knew all about me! He speaks of living water and eternal life. What I say is true! He is still there! If you hurry, surely you will see for yourself! Has the Messiah come to Sychar?"

Some of the women turned and left without a word as Rachel approached. Others pretended to ignore her, keeping their eyes on the fruit and vegetables in the market bins. It was the men who questioned her, "What do you mean, he knew all about you?"

"He said I had five husbands and the man I am with is not my husband!"

A woman counting figs curled her shoulders and shook her head in disgust.

A man replied, "A Jewish prophet? He knows your sin, and yet he speaks to you? I will go. I will see for myself!"

Another replied, "I will go too." Turning to Rachel he said, "Be certain, Rachel. If you are lying, you will pay dearly!"

First the two, then a third and a fourth man walked off. Soon most of the villagers, even the women walked out to see this prophet at the well. As they gathered, Jesus stood up and said, "Friends, there is shade. Do not stand under the hot sun. Sit and listen."

The disciples stood and moved off by the well as the people of Sychar gathered to sit at Jesus' feet. Rachel followed them out and stood a way off. She watched Jesus stretch his arms open, smiling at the people of Sychar.

Jesus began to teach, "The kingdom of God is like a pearl of great value..."

Rachel stared at Jesus and thought, *A Jew, a prophet, here in Sychar? He knows our sin. He knows what we have done, yet he welcomes us? Look how he smiles! His voice is tender. Could it be true? Is that his love I feel?*

The afternoon passed by. The sun was low on the horizon. One of the village elder's stood up, "Teacher, the day is late. We would hear more from you. Please, stay with us this night. Let us show you the hospitality of our village. Come to my house, and your disciples. We will provide for them as well. You must eat and have a safe place to sleep. I know it is not right in the eyes of the Jews to have dealings with Samaritans, but please, do us this honor."

Jesus stood up and lifted one arm towards the city gate. "We will follow. Your hospitality is welcome."

The disciples looked at each other and without word, followed Jesus as he walked alongside the city elder. Slowly the crowd of Samaritans made their way back to their homes. Rachel stood at the side of the road watching her neighbors file by.

The first men who spoke to her in the market stopped and chided her. "It is no longer because of what you said that we believe. For we have heard for ourselves and know that he indeed is the Savior of the world."

At that moment, Jesus stopped and turned around. "Rachel. Are you coming? Draw your water and follow me."

The water jug! Rachel hurried to the well, drew her water jug, lifted it onto her shoulder and walked briskly home.

Rachel had just placed the jug in the door when the man returned. "What was the commotion at the well?" he asked as he took a small pouch of coins and hid it in the bed post.

"Jesus. A Jew and he a prophet, has come to Sychar. He taught at the well and now has come to stay with us and teach…"

"He will not stay in this house," the man interrupted.

"The elder has invited him to stay. I am going to hear him again."

"My dinner!" the man shouted.

"Feed yourself—or come with me. Hear what he has to say. Never has any man spoken like him in Sychar or all of Samaria. He is a prophet! I believe he is the Messiah!"

"I am hungry. I have no interest in your Messiah. Go if you must; but come home quickly. I have strong desires that only you satisfy."

Rachel stopped at the door, turned and looked at the man she lived with. "If you will not come—if you will not change, I have no need or desire for you. This is my house. I don't want to find you here when I return. Things have changed. I have changed. Go."

Rachel took a small water jar, a basin and a towel and went out into the dusk. She hurried to the house of the village elder where Jesus and his disciples were gathered at the door. Jesus was speaking to the elder as the disciples removed their sandals and washed their feet. Rachel came up behind Jesus and gently pulled him to a bench at the door where he sat down. Wordlessly, she unstrapped his sandals, brushed away the manure, dirt and dust caked to his feet. Then she poured clean water and wiped away the mud, pouring a second time to rinse them clean. Kneeling before him she dried his feet with the towel. She then washed his sandals and tied them on his feet.

The elder's face burned red with anger. "Woman! This is not your place!"

Jesus lifted the palms of his hand and shook his head softly while smiling. His voice gentle, he said, "Leave her alone. Allow her this gift."

Jesus looked down, "Rachel."

Again, their eyes met as Rachel looked up into his face. "Your servant, Lord."

"You have chosen well. Do not return to your sin. The kingdom of God is before you." Rachel's eyes remained fixed on his and slowly tears welled up in her eyes as a smile emerged from her lips. She drank in his compassion as he said, "Come inside and listen."

The guests inside stopped talking and watched as Rachel followed Jesus and sat down at his feet. Jesus looked at the guests staring at Rachel and began to teach. "What man among you, if he has a hundred sheep and has lost one of them, does not leave the ninety-nine in the open pasture, and go after the one which is lost until he finds it? And when he has found it, he lays it on his shoulders, rejoicing. And when he comes home, he calls together his friends and his neighbors, saying to them, 'Rejoice with me, for I have found my sheep which was lost!'"

The guests looked at Rachel sitting quietly before Jesus. One by one they gathered around the table set before Jesus and sat down in silence. Jesus was hungry. He took a piece of bread, blessed it and ate his first meal since breakfast.

He took a drink of the wine and glanced to the wealthy village elder and then looking at each of the guests he continued to teach, "A certain man had two sons; and the younger of them said to his father, 'Father, give me the share of the estate that falls to me.' And he divided his wealth between them. And not many days later, the younger son gathered everything together and went on a journey into a different country, and there he squandered his estate with loose living."

Every ear was listening as Jesus continued, "Now when he spent everything, a severe famine occurred in that country, and he began to be in need. He went and attached himself to one of the citizens of that country, and he sent him into his fields to feed swine. He was longing to fill his stomach with the pods that the swine were eating, and no one was giving anything to him."

Jesus took another bite of bread and a drink of wine, smiled briefly and continued, "But when he came to his senses, he said, 'How many of my father's hired men have more than enough bread, but I am dying here of hunger! I will get up and go to my father, and will say to him, 'Father, I have sinned against heaven and in your sight. I am no longer worthy to be called your son; make me as one of your hired men.' And he got up and came to his father. But while he was still a long way off, his father saw him and felt compassion for him and ran and embraced him and kissed him."

The room was silent. A few guests took a sip of wine while Jesus paused. He continued, "The son said to him, 'Father, I have sinned against heaven and in your sight; I am no longer worthy to be called your son.' But the father said to his servants, 'Quickly, bring out the best robe and put it on him, and put a ring on his hand and sandals on his feet; and bring the fatted calf, kill it, and let us eat and be merry, for this son of mine was dead and has come to life again; he was lost and has been found. And they began to be merry."

Rachel glanced up for just a moment, but quickly lowered her face and wiped a tear from her eye. The guests glanced about nodding politely and returned to their meal.

They were startled by the earnestness in Jesus' voice as he spoke louder. "Now his older son..."

Eyes again turned to Jesus. "...was in the field, and when he came and approached the house, he heard music and dancing. He summoned one of the servants and asked what these things might be. And he said to him, 'Your brother has come, and your father has killed the fattened calf, because he has received him back safe and sound.' But he became very angry and was not willing to go in. His father came out begged him, but he answered his father, 'Look! For so many years I have been serving you, and I have never neglected a command of yours; and yet you have never given me a kid that I might be merry with my friends; but this son of yours came, who has devoured your wealth with harlots, and you killed the fattened calf for him."

Jesus took a deep breath and opened his arms and went on, "My child, you have always been with me and all that is mine is yours. But we had to be merry and rejoice, for this brother of yours was dead and has begun to live and was lost and has been found."

No one questioned Jesus on his teaching.

The guests finished their meal and began to leave. The wealthy elder spoke up. "We would hear more of your teaching tomorrow. Please stay with us and…"

Jesus nodded, "I will stay and teach under the tree by the well."

Jesus and the disciples were provided rugs and mats and made themselves comfortable in the sheltered courtyard of the elder's house. The young disciple, John, laying down looking at the stars above quietly said to his older brother James, "The master shares the same message with the Samaritans as that he shares with the Jews."

Jesus heard John, whom he loved, and said, "The well is indeed the very one dug by the patriarch Jacob to whom the father gave the name Israel. They have not forgotten. They do not worship in the Temple and they do not follow the law of Moses as they should. Does the father love them any less than their brothers who worship in the temple but also corrupt the law of Moses? John, have I not said, 'God is Spirit and those who worship Him will worship Him in spirit and in truth?'"

John asked, "Will you go to the gentiles too?"

Jesus answered, "There shall be a light to the gentiles. The Father does not wish that any be lost but that all should come to repentance."

John thought about Jesus' words and then said softly, "The woman. Did you come here for the woman or all the villagers?"

John could not see Jesus smile.

Rachel returned to her house, her head spinning, but a radiant smile glowing from her face. When she opened her door, she saw a candle lit on the table and the man seated there with a cup of wine. "You're back at last! Lurking in the shadows outside the elder's house no doubt."

Rachel's smile disappeared. "I told you to leave!"

She stood inside the door and held it open for him. "Go! Get out and never come back!"

The man stared at her for a moment and said, "You're serious." He took a deep breath as anger swept across his brow. "If I leave, I am not coming back!" he shouted.

"Good! Never come back. That is what I have told you. Now go. Take what you have stolen and go!"

The man stood up, went to his hiding place and took several pouches of money. He stopped and looked at Rachel. "You've changed. Do you really think that you can become a respectable woman?"

"Go!"

"It's the Jew. The teacher. What has he said? You will never get him into your bed!"

Rachel stood holding the door, "Go."

The man walked out into the chilled night air and Rachel closed and barred the door behind him.

The next morning, Rachel rose early and went to the well while the morning was yet cool. She smiled as she walked and did not feel the weight of the water jug on her shoulder. Most of the women stopped talking as she walked by and none addressed her, still she smiled, walked to the well, drew her water and returned home.

When the crowd following Jesus and the disciples walked past her house, she opened her door and walked along with them. She sat near the front as they assembled under the tree and Jesus began to teach, "Blessed are you who are poor, for yours is the kingdom of God. Blessed are you who hunger now, for you shall be satisfied. Blessed are you who weep now, for you shall laugh. Blessed are you when men hate you, and ostracize you, and cast insults at you, and spurn your name as evil, for the sake of the Son of Man."

Jesus scanned the crowd and then looked down to Rachel. "Be glad in that day, and leap for joy, for behold you reward is great in heaven; for in the same way their fathers used to treat the prophets."

Looking up across the confused faces he said, "But woe to you who are rich, for you are receiving your comfort in full. Woe to you who are well fed now, for you shall be hungry. Woe to you who laugh now, for you shall morn and weep. Woe to you when all men speak well of you, for in the same way their fathers treated the false prophets. But I say to you who hear, love your enemies, do good to those who hate you, bless those who curse you, pray for those who mistreat you. Whoever hits you on the cheek, offer him the other also, and whoever takes away your coat, do not withhold your shirt from him either."

Jesus paused and looked at a man standing alone at the back of the crowd. The man was not there the first day. "Give to everyone who asks of you, and whoever takes away what is yours, do not demand it back. And just as you want people to treat you, treat them in the same way. And if you love those who love you, what credit is that? But love your enemies and do good and lend, expecting nothing in return, and your reward will be great, and you will be sons of the Most High; for He Himself is kind to ungrateful and evil men. Be merciful just as your Father is merciful."

Only the sound of the light breeze through the leaves could be heard. Even the birds were silent. Every eye was fixed on Jesus. Everyone there felt their heart penetrated by his gaze. Jesus sighed and said, "And do not judge…"

He paused and smiled warmly, "Do not judge and you will not be judged; and do not condemn and you will not be condemned; pardon and you will be pardoned."

Jesus opened his arms and said with a smile in his voice, "Give and it will be given to you; good measure, pressed down, shaken together, running over, they will pour into your lap. For by your standard of measure it will be measured to you in return."

Jesus taught until the sun was high in the sky and the heat became heavy upon them. Peter said, "Lord send them home that they take refreshment and shelter from the heat, for the sun is high and no one dare draw water while you speak."

Jesus looked up to the sun just as he had as they approached Sychar the day before and he nodded to Peter. "Let us go into the city with them, for my time is not yet finished here."

Peter addressed the crowd. "Please, brothers and sisters go home and take refreshment. The Rabbi has more to teach you."

The citizens of Sychar stood and began making their way towards the city, speaking and debating what they heard as they walked. The elder's wife came alongside Rachel and said, "It is a good thing you told us about the teacher. Truly he is a prophet. What more did he tell you? I feel the power of his words, but there is much I do not understand."

When they reached the gate of the city near Rachel's house, the elder's wife said, "Please, come with me, I would hear more."

Jesus taught again in the afternoon. He spoke of not coveting and not laying up treasures on earth and warned them against greed. He comforted them against worry and encouraged their faith in a loving heavenly Father. He spoke of the power of faith as small as the mustard seed and doing the master's will. He spoke of division and signs of the times to come. Again, and again he shared his vision of the coming Kingdom and the love and joy it would bring.

He challenged them, "When you give a luncheon or a dinner, do not invite your friends or your brothers or your relatives or your rich neighbors, lest they also invite you in return, and repayment come to you. But when you give a reception, invite the poor, the crippled, the lame the blind, and you will be blessed since they do not have means to repay you; for you will be repaid at the resurrection of the righteous."

When Rachel went home that evening, the man was waiting outside her door. "Forgive me Rachel. I understand now. Would you permit me to court you—honorably?"

Rachel looked at the man before standing before her, clean and sober.

"I have returned all that I have stolen—I will never again steal, I... I want a new life—to walk with you and seek the kingdom Jesus speaks of."

Rachel stared in silence while he stood face to the ground. "If you have truly repented... I might allow an honest man—a righteous man to call on me."

That night a great banquet was prepared for Jesus and his disciples. At the table Jesus turned to the those standing nearby and said, "When you are invited to a wedding feast, do not take the seat of honor. Lest someone more distinguished than you may have been invited by him, and he who invited you both come and say to you, 'Give your place to this man and then in disgrace you proceed to occupy the last place. But when you are invited, go and sit at the last place, that when the one who has invited you comes, he may say to you, 'Friend, move up higher. For everyone who exalts himself will be humbled; and he who humbles himself will be exalted."

The guests sat as they pondered this teacher who spoke in parables and contradictions. Mesmerized they listened as he told the story of a wealthy king who persisted with much determination to fill a great hall to honor the marriage of his son. At the end of the banquet, Jesus rose, thanked his host and said he would resume his journey to Galilee in the morning.

Peter said to Jesus in the nighttime quiet of the courtyard, "The people do not understand your parables."

"Peter, do you not remember the parable of the seed which I explained to you? The seed has been planted in the soil of Sychar. It will grow in the good soil. To you and to whosoever's heart where it grows, it has been granted to know the mysteries of the kingdom of heaven. But where it dies or does not sprout, in their case the prophecy of Isaiah is being fulfilled, which says, 'Hearing you will hear and shall not understand, and seeing you will see and not perceive.' But blessed are your eyes and the eyes of all who see, and your ears and all whose ears hear, because they hear. For truly I say to you that many prophets desired to see what you see and did not see it and hear the words you hear but did not hear them."

On the third day Jesus arose and departed the city of Sychar with his disciples. Rachel heard the commotion of the people following Jesus as they made their way past her house. She quickly covered her head with her scarf and was out the door. As Jesus passed through the city gate, Rachel called out, "Rabbi, before you leave, please... please teach us to pray!"

Jesus smiled. He stopped, turned around and opened his arms. "Rachel come, come all of you and listen."

Rachel walked boldly forward, and the crowd followed her. As she stood before him, he spoke loudly but his eyes were on Rachel. "When you pray, say 'Father, hallowed be your name. Your kingdom come; your will be done. Give us each day our daily bread. And forgive us our sins as we ourselves forgive everyone indebted to us. And do not bring us to the time of trial."

When Jesus finished, he turned and walked north towards Galilee. Rachel stood and watched him walk away. Several of the women came alongside her and one said, "I have never met anyone like him. But I wonder... tell us, Rachel, you seem to understand, in all of his teachings, what would he have us learn?"

Rachel did not turn her eyes from Jesus, but answered softly, "God loves me. He loves each and every one of us."

Rachel turned to the women and smiled warmly. "Trust Him. Know that it is His desire that we love Him, and He asks that we love each other as well."

Rachel turned and smiled at the women, "Come, we must draw our water before it is too hot."

Two hours later another Samaritan village appeared on the horizon. Jesus closed his eyes as before, looking to heaven. Peter asked, "Lord, shall we go into the city?"

Jesus sighed. "You may enter if you wish and ask if they will listen, but they will not hear you. They will send you away."

Peter looked into Jesus' face and said, "It was for her. We came to Sychar for the woman at the well."

Jesus smiled and said, "A blessed woman. Her seed will return more than a hundred-fold."

AUTHOR BIOGRAPHIES

Stacey Venzel

Stacey Venzel is a published author, freelance writer, teacher, actress, and zoologist. She finds joy in the small things in life and often creates opportunities to merge her many passions. Writing has helped her heal from many past traumas and always remains an outlet to express herself free from rules. Stacey resides in the Hudson Valley in New York.

J.W. Capek

J.W. Capek has combined storytelling with collecting characters through the avenues of grandmothers' wonderful stories, storytime at the library, reader's theatre, and working in Community Theatre. Teaching high school Social Studies and Math could always be enhanced with stories. Predating social media, JWC developed the Senior to Senior Intergenerational Telecommunications project allowing students to communicate globally with senior citizens. Now living in the Pacific Northwest, JWC tells a science fiction tale—The Deerwhere Saga peopled with Quantum Computers, and three unique genders: Female, Male, and Uniale.

Amber Rainey

A mom first in all things she does, Amber just happens to also be an author, actor, and award-winning filmmaker. She lives in Texas with her engineer husband, precocious son, and two cats, who vie for her lap while she writes. Amber has yet to find a medium she doesn't enjoy so she writes novels, short stories, and screenplays. Her first novel, *Eternal Willow*, can be found online at Amazon. You can visit www.amberrainey.com and www.tiny.cc/amberrainey for more about Amber and her work.

Angela Faro

Angela Faro is an artisan of many skills who resides in Washington State. She is an author, an award-winning filmmaker and actress, a musician, singer, and journalist. Her previous writing includes a novelization of the *Ghost Sniffers, Inc.* episode *Wild Things Waking*, various short stories, poetry, and articles for *Arts Ex Machina Magazine* and a reoccurring column in the *Northwest Karaoke & Entertainment Guide* called *The NW Film Focus*.

David Fuller

David Fuller is a freelance writer for the tabletop games industry. When he's not working on a book or chasing his four kids around, he's streaming RPGs at: Twitch.tv/gamerbehindtherows.

Marshall Miller

After retiring as a Senior Special Agent/Federal Criminal Investigator, Marshall found a second career in writing and has a published four book series called THE TSCHAAA INFESTATION. These in-depth science fiction/speculative fiction works examine the human condition, and what people would do to survive when threatened with being eaten by an invading intelligent alien species. His thirty years of law enforcement experience and world travel provides him with the basis for the many varied characters which populate his literary works, demonstrating the good, the bad, and the ugly.

Elaina Gonzales-Blanton

Elaina is Texas born, and moved to Kitsap County in Washington State thirty years ago this September. She is a wife, a mother, a scholar of history and government studies, and an avid animal lover. Elaina lost her father two and a half years ago to Alzheimer's disease and has found healing through music and in writing her story and speaking her truth.

Eliza Loeb

Eliza stepped in to the writing field in 2018, beginning with the *Prompt Anthology* for Blue Forge Press. Originally born on Guam, they had spent their life reading, writing and creating with many artistic influences. Today, Eliza channels their creativity and experiences through their writing. A recently published piece of Eliza Loeb's work can be found on Amazon in the horror anthology *Unnerving*. For those of you who would like to see the human behind the writer, feel free to follow Eliza on Tumbler at imelizaloeb.tumblr.com.

Susan Nordman

Susan Nordman is an author in love with both Science Fiction and the Pacific Northwest. Born into a military family, she began life in Aurora, Colorado, spent most of her childhood in England before finally ending up in Gig Harbor, Washington. Susan earned a bachelor's degree in creative writing. Except for publishing a few poems which won awards for Editor's Choice, Merit and honorable mentions, she did absolutely nothing with her writing for the next thirty years. That's all changed! With her first short story published in *Enduring*, she is currently adding the final touches to *Ascension – Book 1 of the Psions of Janus*, and another book in a different series titled *The Accidental Alien*. She is also co-authoring a trilogy with her father Vern Nordman, author of *Uncle Sam, My Sailor and Me.*

David Martyn

David Martyn lives in Gig Harbor, Washington with his wife Karen. Retired from a career in the Maritime Industry, he can keep watch over ships passing to and from Tacoma. David writes Christian fiction. He has authored three books in the Hall of Faith series: "The Praise Singer: A Disciple of Melchizedek," "The Oak of Weeping," and "The Epistle: A Story of the Early Church." He has also authored a historical fiction "Called Into Service—a Robert Curtis Mystery."